STILL BLACK

Tammy Ferebee

STILL BLACK

Copyright © 2022 by Tammy Ferebee

Cover design by Molly Van Roekel
Interior design and layout by Shahinur Alam
ISBN-13: 978-0-9966292-3-2

www.tammyferebee.com

First Edition

I may want to slap you at least once a day. I may find some of your jokes too corny to repeat.

I may take power naps while you're telling me one of your three-hour-long stories. But I never want to lose this friendship. Your support means the world to me, and so does our bond. Thanks for everything, T. Forever my ace boon coon!

PROLOG

His dried, bloody handprint has permanently stained my favorite Malcolm X shirt. I stare at it, at where his hand was, bewildered by my feelings. I had always believed that committing such an act would leave one, especially me, burdened by guilt, ultimately leading to an overwhelming feeling of remorse. But I don't feel either. Unexpectedly, I'm showered with relief, as though I've done my part in cleaning up the world. Maybe I've never truly known myself or my capabilities, or maybe it's simply too soon for me to trust anything I'm feeling.

Eyes still on his blood, I realize I'll never get to wear this shirt again. After *they* force me to remove it, it'll likely only reappear once more, as evidence during my inevitable trial. Following the reading of a verdict I won't be surprised by, it'll be stored, forever stained.

I sit, cuffed, awaiting an officer to enter the vehicle and drive me to my new home, finished with concrete walls. As I wait, more patient than I've ever been, I look out the window, an opportunity I'm not likely to have again after this joyless ride.

There she is. The most reliable bulletproof vest. I'm in this backseat, with life in my body, because of *her*. Nowadays, that's not common. I'm one of the lucky ones who has actually survived an arrest. I'm breathing, no bullets in my body, not the victim of a fatal chokehold, not lying lifelessly on the concrete from a deadly beating. I'm here, I'm Black, I'm still alive, but the reason why will take some time to fully digest.

BLACK

I never pray for sunshine. A warm, cloudy afternoon is a gift to me, and we plan to take full advantage of this one. School let out three hours early so teachers could submit their third-quarter grades, leaving us to enjoy the rest of this Friday afternoon doing whatever we choose. Our choice, a one-on-one game of basketball, at home, without an audience. No loud cheers, no chanting of my brother's name, our girls not in attendance. Just us.

Andrew tosses his basketball from one hand to the other as we walk. "Bruh, I've been waiting to destroy you in a game of one-on-one."

I've been waiting for this beating, too. Only older than me by one year, Drew performs light-years ahead of me on the court, earning him quite the fan base at our high school. No matter how hard he's worked with me or how many clinics I've dedicated my free time to, the fluidity of his movements and his ability to effortlessly hit buckets makes me look like a first-year amateur. He plays at a level I admire, but have never aspired to reach. Becoming the next Jaylen Fisher has never been on my wish list, but the court remains another home for me. For us. It's where we share secrets, talk shit, and it's my favorite place to release whatever has hidden itself inside me.

"You ain't destroying shit, bruh," I throw back, knowing my only chance of winning would be an NBA star replacing me. "Don't cry when I dunk on you."

"Dunk on what, fool? Can you touch the net yet?"

"Fuck you." I try to grab the ball.

Drew twists his body quickly, the ball gripped firmly between his hands.

"Damn," I say, under my breath.

"Still too slow, little brother. Too short, and too slow."

I chuckle, and we continue down the sidewalk, my five-foot-nine next to his six-foot-three.

"You give any thought to what coach brought up?"

"Nah." I shake my head. "I don't have the time."

"Make the time, Malachi. Sign up with me to help run clinics for the kids at the rec center, and get those hours now. Don't wait until your senior year like I did. I should be chillin', but I'm scrabbling to get everything done before graduation."

"Can't," I tell him again. "If I run clinics, that's less time I have to offer online peer support.

That's less time I have to put toward my film projects and to improve on my editing."

"How are things with the support group?"

"Hard, and I'm just listening. They're the ones actually experiencing bullying and isolation because of how they look. Here I am with a girlfriend, a team, support all around me. The life they wish they had, I have."

"But your life ain't perfect. You have hardships too. Y'all talk about race, right?"

I nod. "It comes up."

"That's worth digging into. You're Black, no matter how white your skin is, which means you were born a target in this country. Talk about that. People around here aren't nasty to you, but who knows what college will be like for you? Are you nervous about what life will be like after high school?" Drew persists. "Tell them. Are you worried about finding another girlfriend if you and Denise don't work out? Open up about that stuff. If there are younger kids in the group, let them know you know what it's like to stand out without wanting to. Don't accidentally separate yourself from them by appearing as though you don't have any problems. Ain't no connecting if you do that."

I nod, instantly remembering our first day of MMA practice many years ago. I walked in alongside my brother, terrified they'd pair me with someone who'd choke me to sleep in seconds, but skillset quickly became the least of my worries.

Before we began warmups, the team was instructed to form a circle on the mat, all of us down on our knees. As newcomers, we were asked to introduce ourselves. As always, Drew spoke up first.

"I'm Andrew!" His pitch was as high as his volume. "This is my little brother, Malachi!" He threw his arm around me. "And nobody better mess with him!"

As the gym erupted in laughter, mostly from the older kids and parents, all eyes rushed my way. Immediately, my stomach sank into the mat beneath me.

"Wait a minute. That's your brother?" another student asked in disbelief. "Is he adopted?"

"No!" Drew jumped from his knees to his feet.

The boy grimaced. "Then why does he look like that?"

"Hey, be respectful," the coach intervened, springing in front of my brother while the boy's mother spoke quietly to her son.

Trembling inside my Gi and feeling like the oddball in the room, my eyes drifted to Pop. With his finger extended, he mouthed, *Speak up. Use your voice.*

After accepting the forced apology from my rude new teammate, I began my personal introduction. As if my appearance hadn't stunned everyone enough, my stutter, which hung around until I was nine, definitely floored them. Some with opened mouths, others with widened eyes, my teammates stared intently as I struggled to get my name out. Curious eyes remained glued to me until Pop broke their focus with his stamp of approval, "I'm proud of you, son."

That day and other similar first encounters don't come up for me too often, because more often than not, inquisitive eyes study my skin tone and yellow hair, not eyes filled with repulsion. Still, on occasion, like most other albinos, I have to answer questions about my appearance, and they're usually asked in front of others without tact.

Making me stand out even more, my family is wrapped in skin as dark as soil. They each have a glow others use makeup and filters to achieve, prompting stinging questions about our relation. True, I may not feel like an outcast at home or school, but the inquisitions other albinos face will never not be a thing in my life either—something I now plan to be more open about, so I can connect with those I want to help.

Sauntering on beneath the sunless sky, I remove my photophobia glasses and give silent thanks to the clouds for doing me a huge favor today. No fear of sunburn this afternoon, and no eye discomfort due to brightness. Today may appear gloomy to most, but this is the only kind of day I can spend time outside in short sleeves, play ball without glasses strapped around my head, and enjoy being out without having to worry if my vulnerable skin is protected enough. It's one of those glorious days my special preparations aren't required.

I nudge Drew. "Pass the rock."

He does, quickly replacing the ball with his vibrating phone. Dribbling as we stroll, I peek over at his eagerly typing fingers.

"Fools are still laughing about it," he mumbles.

"About what?"

"Sneaking out last night. Gettin' lit."

"Wish I had been there."

"I invited you, but you had to edit your Malcolm X project."

"I don't regret staying in. I had to get that B up to an A. Just wish I could've seen you out of your damn mind."

Drew cuts his eyes at me.

"Feel sick at all today?" I ask.

"No, Mama. It was weed, not heroin."

I chuckle. "How'd y'all smoke it?"

"Gravity bong."

"You like it?"

He shakes his head. "Can't say the feeling is something I need to feel again. I only hit it twice, and damn! Chest was on fire. Throat was burning. Time got weird." He slides his phone back in his pocket. "I would close my eyes for two minutes, but it would feel like four hours. And I kept thinking about the most pointless shit. Do you know I really sat there philosophizing why radishes grow underground?"

I burst into laughter.

"I mean, who the fuck cares? I don't even eat radishes."

We both crack up.

"It was an interesting first experience, but it ain't for me."

I shrug. "Everyone reacts differently to drinking and smoking."

"Just make sure if you get curious again, I'm the one there with you. You might love Denise and all that, but she shouldn't have let you walk home after drinking. She should've called me. You could've stumbled into the street or something."

I sigh. "I know, Pop. She thought it was cool because I was leaving on foot. We talked about it. Won't happen again."

Drew, without another word, slumps over in a fit of hysterical laughter.

I stop bouncing the ball, run my hand across my unpicked bush. "What?"

"Just thinking about your half-drunk ass doing the robot while Pop was yelling at you. You gotta be out your mind to act the fool when Pop is talking. You looked so stupid, even he had to laugh."

I toss him back the ball, the blur of the memory making me laugh at myself. "Good times, man. Never again, though. The hangover was worse than Pop's punishment."

We hang a left onto our street, and right away, darkness befalls us, robbing us of our smiles. Up until recently, just arriving at the corner warmed us with a feeling that can only be described as *home*. In our colorful, Southern, suburban neighborhood, we're surrounded by family from all backgrounds. Our Black neighbors, white neighbors, Latino neighbors, and even the pretty reserved Asian American family who moved in a year ago, all welcome and treat us with kindness, as though we're their own. We attribute their adoration to our behavior. We've never been troublemakers, we help the elders, often without accepting pay, and always clean up after Rocko when we take him on walks. We respectfully greet every neighbor we pass, as we've been taught to—well, everyone except the Dicksons; a father and son duo, the newest to settle here.

When the Dicksons moved in two months ago, it felt more like an invasion. They made it clear from the moment they moved in that they didn't like us, and we had a pretty good idea as to why. They spoke cheerily to many, but we couldn't help but notice minorities didn't make their cut. Their icy glares, refusal to respond to a courteous *hello,* and antagonistic comments toward *us* said plenty, but nothing screamed louder than their newest choice of home décor—an oversized

Confederate Flag draping the front door of their rented property, a house we used to visit.

Our street is as colorful as the flowers that give our homes more curb appeal, yet racists decided to settle here. Mama warned Mr. Thompson that renting his place could possibly bring in the wrong crowd. I think she was worried about partiers or careless tenants not taking care of her friend's property. None of us expected who or *what* we got.

As Drew and I head up the sidewalk, drawing nearer to the flag almost the entire neighborhood wants to burn, Bennett, not much older than us, leers from the porch. With one foot on the floor for support and the other propped up on the white railing stretched out in front of him, he rocks back and forth on the two back legs of a chair Mr. Thompson used to greet us from. With each step we take, his brows pull down further into a scowl.

I typically go out of my way to avoid eye contact with the Dicksons, as I see angry stare-offs increasing the likelihood of a dangerous confrontation. But not Andrew. He always looks Bennett and his father right in the eye. He doesn't say what's on his mind, doesn't incite violence, but my brother never lowers his head when he walks by, never gives them any pleasure in believing he's afraid of them. I, on the other hand, don't care what they believe. I know my reactions to their ignorance could result in harsh punishment, while theirs could easily be found forgivable in the eyes of the law, even if they are the aggressors.

9

The front two legs of the chair hit the wooden porch floor. "Stay the hell off my grass!" Bennett shouts, jumping to his feet.

I take a quick glance down. Each of our feet is on the sidewalk.

"Ain't nobody on your damn grass!" Drew shoots back.

"Y'all just keep on walking!" Ms. Anna hollers from beneath her awning next door. "Ignore him. He's just looking for trouble." Revulsion narrows her eyes as they look to Bennett. "It's a damn shame that in this day and age, people still act like you. Leave them damn boys alone. They're on the sidewalk. I reckon you think you own everything, but the sidewalk don't belong to you." She waves her finger as she speaks. "That porch you're standing on don't even belong to you."

With one hand, Bennett finger combs his jet-black, shoulder-length hair. With the other, he curses Ms. Anna.

"Are you fucking crazy?" Drew snaps, dropping his basketball and stepping toward Bennett, now standing on his grass. "Respect your elders! Don't ever put your middle finger up at Ms. Anna! I'll drag your ass down those stairs!"

I grab my brother, his fists clenched and ready to strike. "Let's go, Drew. He's not worth it."

Drew pulls away from me. "You're a fucking coward! Step off that porch and put your middle finger in my face!"

I grab my brother again, prepared to use a Jiu Jitsu take down on him if I have to, anything to prevent this fight that he'll ultimately lose, even if he does beat Bennett's ass.

"Go on, baby. Go on home." Ms. Anna's voice is as kind as her heart. "Don't let nobody steal your joy. Honey, I've crossed too many of him in my day to be worried about him giving me the finger. Don't worry about me. Just go on home."

Drew stands, his chest rising and falling at an unhealthy rate, fists still ready to swing, my hands gripping his triceps, prepared to pull him back should he decide to continue toward Bennett.

"Go on, baby," Ms. Anna repeats, her age giving her an authority we fully respect.

Drew finally steps back, sights still locked on Bennett, his rage forcing veins to protrude throughout his arms.

I stare ahead, watch as Bennett bends forward, and rests his elbows on the porch railing. Pleased at the reaction he's receiving, the corners of his lips slowly rise into a diabolical grin. His eyes, which look pitch black from here, are on my brother, further provoking him. Without even blinking, he extends his right arm, and with his index and middle finger, he beckons Drew forward.

"Let's go!" I plead again, louder this time.

Drew takes a couple of steps back. Now, on the sidewalk again, he turns his attention to Ms.

Anna. "I apologize for using profanity in front of you. It won't happen again."

"Go on home, baby. Don't you worry about it. I know where your heart is."

"And I'll be here in the morning to cut this for you," Drew says, pointing at her fast-growing lawn.

"Thank you, baby. Get on home now. Please, for me. Both of you."

I grab Drew's ball and silently walk beside my brother with fire coursing through me. Bennett was desperate to start a fight, and for Andrew, there was no better way to start one than by disrespecting Ms. Anna. We weren't raised to be insolent, most definitely not to our elders. We also weren't taught to stand by and allow a woman to be victimized. Disrespect toward Ms. Anna was a much bigger trigger for my brother than Bennett yelling directly at us.

Bennett has been referred to as coward by some of the others in the neighborhood, but I don't view him that way. He makes calling sounds to our dog and antagonizes us from the safety of his rented porch for a reason. He wants a fight – or worse – to take place, but he needs us to come to him, to strike first, to look like the aggressors. They see a coward, and on some level, I do too. But I mostly see a bigoted strategist. He wants to hurt one of us, but he's plotting out his victim story in advance. He's making sure he can claim self-defense.

We make it home and are promptly greeted by Rocko. His 110-pound, black and brown muscular frame circles us eagerly. Repeatedly, he nudges us both with his head, thrilled to see us and anxious to be petted, but our moods don't match his. We both give him a quick pat and move past him, through the kitchen and into the living room. On our sectional, Mama is stretched out with her head resting in Pop's lap. Playing on our television is *Beloved*. No doubt, Mama picked what they'd spend the afternoon watching. I don't know how she conned Pop into watching one of her favorites again, but she managed to get her way, as she has many times before.

"What y'all doing home so early?"

"Half-day, Pop," I answer, bending to place Drew's ball on the floor. "It's the end of the third marking period."

"Something wrong with your grades?" Pop eyes Andrew.

"No, sir."

Mama rises to her feet, walks over, and hugs me before wrapping Andrew in her arms. "Something is wrong," she states surely.

"Bennett," I say.

Pop's head falls in frustration as Mama releases a ferocious growl. "I'm so damn tired of them. So. Damn. Tired."

The Dicksons may not have broken into our home, may not have physically struck us, may not have called us *niggers* as we passed by, but their constant targeting because of our race has stirred parts of us we know could get us into trouble.

"I pray every night that they move. It's crazy how two people can make an entire neighborhood no longer feel like home, but like…" Mama sighs. "Like…" I watch as she mentally searches for the right word.

"Like a prison," Drew says, finishing her statement. "I feel trapped, stuck with people I hate."

"This ain't no prison," Pop states, rising to his feet and swiftly moving closer to my brother. "This is your home. Don't you ever let nobody make you feel like you're trapped. Don't let people in there." Pop points to Drew's head, his eyes on my brother's. "You let people inside your mind, to plague your thoughts, and they win no matter what. Know why? Because all that rent-free space you give them just makes you ruminate. The longer you sit, thinking about the things they've said, done, or even may do, the closer they get to what it is they really want. And we all know what that is, don't we?"

Mama rubs Drew's back.

"For you to dip your toe over the line just enough for them to call the cops, fire a shot, or draw a blade," Pop says, answering his own question. "Don't let that idiot or his father get inside your head. Don't give them ownership over you. This is just a taste of what's out there, son. I've dealt with more Dicksons in my day than I can count. Yeah, we go through times when things seem okay, but over the past few years, countless white people have unmasked again and gotten a lot more comfortable showing how they really feel about *us*."

"Mm-hmm." Mama nods.

"Well, let them feel how they want to feel, son. Let them think what they want to think. Walk right on by them with your head held high. Now, I'm not telling you not to defend yourself if need be." Pop shakes his head. "I'm telling you not to let this anger consume you. I'm telling you not to overthink yourself into swinging first or exploding. It's a tall order, I know. It takes a lot to be able to do that, but you can, Andrew. You're a Black man!" Pop states loudly. "What's a Black man?" he asks, his volume still high, his question directed at the both of us.

"Strength," we answer in unison.

I quickly glance at Mama as she nods again, always proud to see that our father's words stick, that we do more than hear, but actually listen.

Pop places his hand on Drew's shoulder, not breaking eye contact. "Strength," Pop repeats. "You were born with it in you, and you're going to need it throughout the rest of your life. No matter how nice we want this world to be, it's never going to be that. It's cold out there, son. Cold," he says again with one slow nod. "But it'd be a lot colder sitting inside a cell because of one angry moment. It'd be a lot colder pushing up daisies."

Drew maintains strong eye contact, a requirement in our home, and listens intently as our father speaks. I listen carefully too, my eyes on a man I often describe as my hero. Though Pop's eyes are on my brother, his words and his messages are meant for the both of us.

"We're a lot alike, Andrew. When I was your age, I was hot-headed as all hell too. That's what scares me and keeps me up at night. I don't want you to make the same mistakes I've made. Mistakes that could've put me in the ground."

Mama grunts, shaking her head.

Pop continues, "I want to cuss them the hell out too. I want to beat some sense into them. I want to do everything you want to do, just to stop them from hurting somebody, because they will," Pop states certainly. "And that someone can't be in this house. You understand me? It can't be one of mine," he states firmly, his voice deepened with love and protection. "It takes a lot of strength for me not to do what I want, but I know how much fun they'd have repaying me for that punch with a bullet."

Drew nods, eyes still locked on our father's.

"The strength I have in me, I know my sons have in them. It's not fair that we have to be the bigger men to save our own lives, but we do. Use what your mama and I gave you so you can be around to have this talk with your son one day."

As wise words continue to leave my father's lips, my mind walks me through a history that should've never been and has yet to be concluded with a solid period. Based on every education I've received, equality has never truly existed, and it's the lives of minorities that are still continuously demeaned, devalued, and dehumanized. After hundreds of years of being enslaved, caged in humiliating human zoos, brutally raped, forced into wet-nursing, publicly lynched, made to fight to the death, and even savagely burned alive, the world is more colorful than it ever was, yet *we're* still somehow found undeserving.

Modern day lynchings have become somewhat of a trend, it seems. Protests occur more regularly than holidays, often following the unjust, brutal murder of a minority. Victims' names are popular hashtags, and like millions of others, I deeply hate that this is common news. It sickens me that we have to have these talks, that our parents have to remind us how to interact with bigots for our own safety. Why is this still a *thing*? Why was it ever?

"Son!" Mama taps me.

My eyes dart to her. My deep thoughts pause.

"Your father is talking to you."

I look at my father. "Sorry, Pop. What were you saying?"

"Andrew and I are going to take Rocko for a walk. You coming?"

Originally, I had planned to spend the afternoon learning a thing, or five, from Andrew, but since our game has been postponed, I decide to stay in and call my girl.

I politely decline before hugging my pop, then fist bump my brother who doesn't look as though he'd welcome an embrace. With Drew's ball in hand, I head up to my room. Behind my closed door, I shoot Denise a text asking if she's free to talk. While waiting, I change.

With my phone in a tight grip, and my glasses pocketed in case the sun decides to shine, I re-enter the living room, dressed for the game, should Drew decide it's back on after returning home. Alone, stretched across our sectional, Mama lies with her phone resting on her chest as she speaks to my grandmother on speakerphone, venting about the neighbors she wouldn't wish on any community. I pass by her and head out back. In one of our lounge chairs, I recline, close my eyes beneath the cloudy sky, and enjoy the truth of the silence.

A breeze cools my face, and I try to do what Grandma always suggests: remain grateful for all I have as opposed to crying about what I don't. Sure, the Dicksons have robbed us of the homey feeling our neighborhood was once known for, but here is still far better than where Grandma is.

Grandma Ida was born and raised in the small town of Dolorville—Southern, unprogressive, and almost entirely Black. While absent of racism, in Dolorville, you're required to be a devout Christian, stand against anything not heterosexual, and be capable of reciting scriptures when randomly quizzed by the church's elders. Almost like cult members, Grandma and her neighbors push outdated beliefs I don't share, only making the silence of this afternoon louder. This is home, feeling more imperfect than ever before, but still possessing so much to be thankful for.

I open my eyes, look from the clouds, and scan my yard. I look at what's ours: land my father is so proud of because his never owned property and wasn't able to leave behind anything for his children, except hope. That hope lives deep inside me. Not only do I hope to be the man my father is, but also to become a legend in the film industry, someday known for my exceptional editing, original screenwriting, and signature directing style. Like my Pop has for us, I aspire to provide a comfortable living for my family, making enough to support basic needs and occasionally spoil my wife, who I hope Denise will someday become.

Still no reply from *her*. I briefly scratch my coarse, more-yellow-than-gold mane, then begin to type a text to Drew, asking which way they decided to walk. As my finger hits send, the sound of barking echoes in the distance, letting me know, they're either almost home or moving slowly. Regardless of direction, it shouldn't be hard to catch up.

I rush back inside, mouth to Mama, *I'll be back,* and wait for her nonverbal seal of approval. With her nod and the blow of a kiss, I turn for the door.

"Malachi!" she calls out, phone still on her chest.

I turn, "Yes?"

"Take an umbrella."

"I'll be fine, Mama."

"Take a damn umbrella," she demands again.

On my way out of the living room, I chuckle as Grandma chews out Mama for swearing. Half-listening to the scolding while searching the kitchen, a distant pop forces me to pause. *What the hell was that? I hope it wasn't someone's tire bursting.*

I peek inside the pantry and find the umbrella hanging from the doorknob. Hand reached out to grab it, several more pops steal my attention, forcing my stomach to drop. I hurry back into the living room and find Mama on her feet. Both of our eyes are wide and on each other.

"Mama, I'll call you back," she says before ending the call.

"Were those gunshots?" I ask, moving toward the front door and pulling it open.

"Probably just kids. Y'all got out of school early, but parents didn't get a half-day. Maybe someone's playing with those popping firework things you guys like to throw on the ground."

Loud screams fill the air, followed by another series of three loud pops, much louder than before with the door now open. Both me and Mama jump, and instinctively, I put my arm out, stopping her from stepping outside and possibly getting hurt.

"Get back, Mama."

"Hell no. My son is out there. My husband is out there."

"Call the police! Get help!" We hear someone shout.

Mama dials 911, and I poke my head out a little further, wanting to run, wanting to see who needs help, as everyone in this whole neighborhood, all but two, are people I care about. No question, with the door open, those weren't pop-its hitting the ground. Pop has taken us shooting enough times to recognize the sound of gunfire. Without a barrier muffling the sound, with screams filling the air, I know someone has been shot, in the middle of the afternoon, in our safe neighborhood.

"Andrew!" We hear cried out.

No time to think. No time to consider imminent danger. I bolt in the direction of the screams, my vision distorted by my tears.

As I briskly move, nothing seems clear. As blurred as my sight, sounds are all combining into incoherent thunders of panic and terror.

Gathered near Ms. Anna's house and the Dicksons' rental, a crowd has formed. As I approach, someone grabs my arms from behind. I pull away, not acknowledging who it is or why they took hold of me. My only goal is to see my father, my brother, and my dog.

On her knees, in her front yard, I spot Ms. Anna. Immediately, my heart stops as my eyes hurriedly run up and down her. Blood isn't leaving her body, staining her clothing and the earth beneath. She's okay, physically at least. Tears stream down her cheeks, and without seeing my brother, I know. I know why his name was hollered out. I know why *help* is needed. I know why there's a hysterical crowd gathered and why sounds of alarm are roaring all around me. He's been shot, multiple times from the sound of it. I can feel it. I can see it in her tears.

No longer moving in a hurry, I pass Ms. Anna's house, each step a struggle. It feels like I'm being weighed down, like I'm walking in shoes full of water. Through tear-filled eyes, I approach a nightmare, one far too disturbing to even be dreamt. Face down, with half his body on the street and his legs on the sidewalk, my big brother, my best friend, lies still.

As my eyes scan the seared skin surrounding the hole in the back of his head, another in his back, and one in his right calf, the echoes of gunshots fire off in my brain. I grab my chest and fall down beside him in his blood. Blood as warm as his flesh still is, as warm as the day.

One hand on Andrew, I claw at my chest with the other. I try to free a breath that needs to escape, but can't get out. I rock back and forth in agony, try to scream, begin beating myself in the chest, rocking violently, gripping my brother's blood-drenched shirt. Then, I hear it. The scream. Not mine. Mama's. My eyes rush to her, and my roar fills the air, mixing in with the sounds of her anguish. Neighbors try to grab her, but she fights, pulls away, cries out deafening shrieks, and pushes out of their arms until she makes it onto the Dicksons' yard.

Mama falls to her knees, on top of *him*, and my eyes follow, pulling in the unimaginable. I shake my head in disbelief and suck in a shaky breath, as my eyes widen at the horror. Not just my brother, but my hero too. My father's body is down, riddled with bullets, and I hadn't noticed. My attention was focused on whose name I heard shouted.

On his back, Pop lies, life still in him, hanging on with a fight I've always admired. The sound of his choking compels me to leave my brother's lifeless body.

Hastily, I move toward my father. A neighbor removes their hand, and I put mine where it was, over the hole in Pop's chest. I encourage him to hold on, to fight, to stay with us, as Mama turns

23

Pop's head to the side, giving the blood an easier exit.

"I…" He chokes, forcing blood to spray from his mouth.

"Don't talk, Pop," I manage to say shakily.

"I…" he attempts again.

"I love you too," Mama whispers, right at his ear.

As Pop continues to choke on his blood and his words, he tries again. "I… I told him to run." Blood mists from his mouth. He gags, cringes in misery.

The race can be felt. He's trying to outrun death, and it's catching up to him.

His body begins to convulse, a snore-like sound escapes him, and his eyes begin to roll upward.

"Pop! Pop!"

Mama's scream pierces my ears and heart. My pop isn't the only one slipping away. He's taking a piece of his queen with him. A piece of me too.

He told Andrew to run away, but he didn't make it. Drew tried to make it back home, to safety, to *us*, but was ruthlessly gunned down, facing away from his attacker, impossible to be perceived as threatening.

I don't want to leave Pop, don't want to leave my mama, but I need to be with my brother. He didn't deserve to be shot down, and he doesn't deserve to lie alone now, whether life is in his body or not.

As I move back over to my brother, kneeling neighbors respectfully back away from him. Following right behind me, Mama crawls over, sobbing, "My baby, my baby, my baby."

She pushes Drew onto his back, and I jolt at the sight of the bloody hole in my brother's forehead. I freeze looking at the exit wound, gag looking at his blood, at the opening the bullet left through, taking his life with it.

Still slightly opened, his eyes are as lifeless as his body. Empty and unseeing, they look off into nothingness, no longer full of hope, confidence, love.

His parted mouth will never reveal a smile again, will never again release loud, contagious laughter.

Mama rests her head on his breathless chest and apologizes endlessly as she weeps. "I'm sorry, baby. You didn't deserve this."

I grab my Mama's hand and bawl with her as my eyes move from my brother, to Pop, and then back to Drew again.

I scream out, release Mama's hand, and push my palm firmly against my heart. Agony slices through me, making my body jerk violently. My screams louden and fear enters me as I'm convinced that heartbreak this devastating is too great to survive, that it will literally shatter my heart and rip the life from my body, right here, right now.

I fall over, outweighed by the burden and overpowered by the hurt. I'm losing a battle no one could prepare for. My father and brother aren't just lying dead in front of me. I'm facing an ending. Life as I know it exists no more.

I push even harder against my heart, trying desperately to hold it in place, convinced of the impossible, that it may actually explode within me.

Beside my brother, in his blood, I lie, eyes closed, hand on my chest, with my torturous new reality intensifying a crippling burning that's spreading throughout my insides. Silently, I pray for relief, to feel no more, to be numbed, even if death is the only way to make that possible. I just need to be able to catch my breath, and for that breath to not be sharp and crushing. This suffering is inhumane.

My heart still feeling like it's only moments from rupture, I shriek. Then, behind closed lids, like a slide show I have no control over, images of my *happy* family appear and tell our story, our story of what was. I see my parents watching films together, my brother and me working out together, my father and me trying to assemble a new piece of furniture. I see my brother, father, and me lying on the floor with hardened clay on our faces, filling the roles as Mama's lab rats as we try out new products for her organic skincare line.

Then, I see myself and my brother excitedly greeting our father after his return home from a night of truck driving, something he enjoyed, but never encouraged us to pursue. I see our huge smiles, full of pure joy, because seeing Pop make it home after driving through the night was always a relief. Though we never stared at our parents kissing, it was impossible to not beam watching Mama run and jump into Pop's arms, welcoming him back warmly, despite him never being away for longer than a few nights. As unwanted images of what we used to have and never will again continue to flash behind my closed eyes, the jagged-edged dagger of grief slowly drives through my gut.

My body twitches painfully as new tears form, as my entire being begs for relief of any sort. But it doesn't come.

I reopen my eyes. I pull in a blurry image of my mother leaning over me and the burning sounds of terror surrounding me. I blink a few times, each time allowing me to see her face more clearly.

Her sorrow falls from her bloodshot eyes. "Don't leave me," she begs, tugging at my body, trying to get me up. "Don't leave me, Malachi. You're all I got left." Her head falls to my broken heart, pushing more tears out of me.

Alone. I didn't want to leave my brother lying lifeless and alone for even a second. Wanting this pain to go away isn't enough to make me toy with the idea of death a second time. My mother being left without any of us is almost more unimaginable than what I'm being forced to face. She needs me.

I place my hand on my mother's head gently. Hurriedly, she sits back up, and her eyes find mine. Sirens scream all around, but Mama's voice is crystal clear. "I need you, son."

She leans down and kisses my forehead. Her fallen tears meet mine. We're in this hole together. We didn't dig it, didn't fall in by our own doing, but we're still here, and it's up to me to get my mama through this. Somehow.

I push into an upright position, wrap my mama in my arms, and hold her firmly as she screams into my chest. My eyes drift back to my father. Her protector, her greatest supporter, her soulmate, has been ripped from her life. It wasn't an unexpected, but forgivable, automobile accident that took him from her. It wasn't cancer, a heart attack, or any other medical condition that he fought, but couldn't beat. It was cold, brutal, merciless murder.

"Sir! Ma'am! Up and back! This is a crime scene!" a deep voice hollers.

I look up, sure there's no way we're being addressed, sure one of my neighbors has gotten too close and is being asked to back up. But what I felt sure of isn't so. The officer, emotionless in face, stands over us, hand on his gun, and repeats again for us to back away.

Mama pulls her face from my chest and looks up at the officer. Rage forces her body to tremble all over. My body reacts the same way.

"Back up? This is my son." She glances at Andrew's bloody body. "My son!"

Mama rises to her feet, and I find the strength to do the same. I move in front of her five-foot frame and meet the eyes of the officer whose height is about the same as mine.

"You back up!" Mama moves from behind me. "How disrespectful can you be? My son and my husband are lying here dead! Don't tell me to back up! Go in that house and rip the racist murderers out by their fucking hair! Drag them to the electric chair where they belong!"

My neighbors bellow in agreement. Cries can be heard all around me, and demands for the officers to arrest Bennett Dickson are hollered heatedly. Others shout for the officers to gun him down the way he did our family while several different voices announce that they're recording, as if phones really have any impact on how officers treat *us*.

"Ma'am, back up! This is a crime scene," he repeats formally, hand still on his gun, seemingly unfazed that our hearts are lying on the ground with blood spilling from their bodies in the middle of the afternoon.

"Don't address my mother with your hand on your piece. Take that energy in that house and arrest the racist motherfucker who did this to my father and brother!"

Sounds of chaos grow, but I refuse to turn around and face my neighbors, my extended but unrelated family. I keep my eyes on the officer, mostly his hand, as it never moves away from his holstered weapon.

I move back in front of Mama, wanting to protect her from whatever may come next. Eyes still on the officer standing before me, my ears take in a deep voice that sounds close. "A dog as well!"

My eyes move in the direction of the voice. Another officer, several feet away, is focused on something before his feet.

Rocko. I hadn't thought about what had happened to him. As much as I love our dog, seeing Drew and my father's bodies didn't leave any room for thoughts of his whereabouts. Unfortunately, I know them now. He's not home, in our yard, awaiting our return. He's not hiding, frightened because of the gunfire. He's here, as still as Drew and Pop. His eyes are open, but there's no life in them.

Mama's nails dig into my arms as her forehead presses into my back. As she bawls, my head drops. *Even our dog.* Undoubtedly, I'd be lying here too, had I joined them on their walk. I don't know how to feel grateful for that. I'm still alive, no bullets lodged in my body, but I'm not whole. I haven't been left unhurt. Neither has my mother. We're victims too.

The chaos, the screaming, the smell of death in the air swallows me. I can hear the shortness of my breath and stumble back.

"Back up!" The officer yells, his saliva spraying in my face.

The grip of Mama's hands suddenly releases my arms. Her body thuds against the ground, and I swing around swiftly.

No time to focus on the out-of-line officer. No time to question how much longer I'll be able to remain on my feet. *Mama.* That's the only concern at the moment. If my back to the officer invites him to shoot me, so be it. I'll go down trying to take care of my queen.

***

As Mama is rushed out of the ambulance and into the emergency department, I follow closely behind, ignoring the voices telling me to stay in the waiting area.

We enter an empty room, and I stand to the side, out of the way, wishing I could hold my mother's hand. Never once have I seen her look so small, so frail.

I close my eyes tightly, pull out my photophobia glasses, and rush to put them on to protect my eyes from the room's bright light. Three nurses surround Mama, throwing out medical terms I've never heard, and begin prepping her for an IV.

31

A doctor enters. His eyes scan Mama and bulge at the amount of blood that has stained her clothing. He then turns to me, looks me over, quickly noticing I'm wearing my own pattern of dried bloodstains.

"My God, son," he says frantically. "What happened?"

What happened?

"I-I-I-I..." My mouth trembles, but no other sounds escape. I suck in a deep breath, stunned by my struggle to get my words out. "Sh-sh-sh-she," I manage to say, recognizing a stutter I haven't heard since elementary school.

I stop trying to get the words out, as I so often used to do from embarrassment. But that's not the case, not today. The hell of this day has forced my silence.

What happened? Too defeated to make another verbal attempt, I let my head fall. Even if I could get the words out, I don't want to state the facts of the day. I just want to hit rewind and be back on the sidewalk laughing with my brother again. I want to re-enter my home, pat Rocko a little longer, and see Mama's head resting in Pop's lap. I don't want to go back years, just hours, if it's even been that long. Time seems so immeasurable all of a sudden.

He quickly glances at the nurses tending to Mama, then looks back at me. "Son, what happened?" he asks again, his hand on my shoulder, just like Pop's was on Drew's earlier. "Do you need help too?"

I lift my head. My light, hazel, golden-green eyes find his. Our complexions are close, only I'm paler. Though lighter than him, this skin won't save me. My African American features reveal a race I'm proud to call my own, but make me the target of so many things my lack of pigment can't save me from.

What happened? The unwarranted destruction of a family. If I were to explain the shooting, I'm sure either he or one of the nurses would naturally ask *why* Drew and Pop were gunned down like rabid animals in the middle of the day. But I doubt the *why* is something they want to hear, face, and have to find an appropriate response to.

Why? That can be explained simply. It can be summed up in one short, but powerful, and somehow threatening word. We're not the first. Sadly, we won't be the last. Our family tragedy came about because my brother and father were one thing. Not criminals. Not ruthless predators. Black.

TIME

There's never enough, but it's always counted on. For my brother, Pop, and Rocko, theirs was unnecessarily cut short.

It's been nearly seven months since we've been inside our home, walked our street, seen our beloved neighbors. After the funeral, Mama couldn't bear returning. Our house was no longer our home, our safe haven. It was empty and cold, even with the two of us in it, and strangely, it felt even emptier, even lonelier, with others around cooking and tending to us.

Almost immediately following the shooting, floral tributes, wreaths, teddy bears, candles, basketballs, and even dog bones started appearing on our lawn. The generous tributes couldn't bring smiles to our faces upon our return from the hospital, but the care was acknowledged and appreciated.

While the flames of jarred white candles danced on our front lawn to honor the lives of our family members, red and blue lights whirled only a few houses away. Officers were still at the scene of the crime when we returned home that night, though we had been informed that the bodies had already been photographed and removed. Shortly before the coroner had arrived to pronounce my family dead at the scene, Bennett, without cuffs on his wrists, but instead a backpack slung over one shoulder, was escorted to a police car. His hands covered his face as my neighbors shouted vicious threats at witnessing the gentle treatment he was receiving. Where he was being driven to was undisclosed, but it most certainly was not jail.

Ms. Anna, our provider of updates, was in our home awaiting our return. She let herself in while we were in the emergency room, as our front door had been left wide open in our state of panic from earlier that afternoon. She prepared food for us and tidied up the kitchen, wanting my mother and me to do nothing more than eat, grieve, and rest. Unfortunately, we couldn't do that. We were angry, broken, in search of answers and justice that we knew we may never get, but tried to hold out hope for. That hope earned us great disappointment. That hope proved to be a disheartening waste of our time.

The news of the murders spread like wildfire, and the gruesome videos of the aftermath began to circulate the following day, igniting a mighty uproar. Over a million people clicked, shared, and watched as Mama and I approached the scene and broke at the sight of pure evil. With every new viewer, every new fallen tear, the temperature of the country climbed higher and higher until a blaze of rage spread across the states. Demands for the death penalty were being tweeted and called into the station. Threats on Bennett Dickson's life were being publicly posted by the minute. Our family tragedy had instantly become a nationwide loss, and the voices of millions created a pressure cooker Bennett and the officers could not escape. Public statements weren't delayed and were shared much sooner than we had all anticipated.

The story the police bought and sold to the media on behalf of Bennett Dickson was that my father trespassed on his property, and the size of our Rottweiler made him feel frightened for his life. Bennett claimed my father walked our out-of-control dog onto his lawn and began taunting and threatening him, prepared to violently finish the argument Bennett accused Andrew of instigating earlier that afternoon. He claimed he was outnumbered and cried emotionless tears in front of news cameras as he uttered the words, "I didn't want to, but I had to protect my life. It's my right."

Ms. Anna's witness statement proved Bennett's story to be a fictitious account, not one word of it true. Though videos didn't capture my family approaching his yard, Ms. Anna's account, which hasn't changed by a single word, stated that my family was walking our dog, following the same route they always did. She stated that my father and brother didn't say anything to Bennett, but rather it was Bennett who initially spoke, yelling obscenities from his porch before snapping his fingers and shaking a bag of chips at Rocko. Ms. Anna described Rocko pulling excitedly toward

Bennett, as he often did toward our other neighbors who would call to him and want to pet him. Though my father demanded that Rocko stop, and even tugged at his leash, Bennett continued to entice him with the snack and even threw a few chips on the ground. The moment my father's feet were pulled onto the Dicksons' rented grass, the bag dropped, and the 40 Smith and Wesson was revealed.

Protests erupted across the country. Millions walked their cities, using their voices to demand justice, not even breaking on rainy days, and continuing throughout the day we laid our loved ones to rest. As millions remained in their cities, marching, signs held high above their heads, wearing shirts with my family members' photos on them, others came to us. Strangers from near and far traveled to pay their respects to my brother and father, people they didn't know personally, but felt so connected to through their unfortunate ending. Side by side, their caskets laid open as slow-moving lines of strangers approached with lowered heads.

Celebrities showed for the viewing, some interested in singing and speaking, others offering financial support, but Mama shook her head. She also refused to allow filming, insisting that funerals are the last moments to see someone and an opportunity to release emotion without fear of a camera catching your most vulnerable moments of heartache. Mama stated that cameras are meant for events people want to remember, and funerals aren't events for strangers to attend.

Grandma surprisingly didn't agree and worked overtime to convince Mama to allow the public to view the bodies. Grandma didn't want the last viewing of Pop and Andrew to be the bloodbath people saw on the disturbing videos that floated around social media. She wanted the world to see them at peace. Grandma felt that if people were being tear-gassed, arrested, and a few unfortunately killed in their peaceful fight for our family, they should be able to view and pay their respects to them in person. Mama eventually gave in and welcomed the world to view the bodies, but she couldn't be persuaded when it came to the funeral service. Her answer was firm and ultimately respected.

Teachers spoke at the funeral, our coaches, our friends, some of our neighbors, including a guilt-stricken Mr. Thompson, who owned the property my family died on. There was no program, no singing, and very little preaching. Mama was too broken for a homegoing celebration and wasn't in the mood for a Sunday service style goodbye. Instead, she provided a safe space for everyone who wanted to speak to have the floor. She allowed everyone who loved Pop and Drew to grieve together and share memories, some of which actually earned a few laughs. None of those laughs belonged to Mama or me, but the sounds of merriment pouring out of those we loved was almost melodic, especially since neither of us had cracked a smile since before the carnage took place on that bloody Friday.

Now, residents of Dolorville, and immediate family members of my grandmother, I'm living in what feels like the past, a time of ignorance, a time of intolerance. I've never more appreciated what used to be my home. I've heard plenty of derogatory words, but have never been anywhere where they're so comfortably used by both adults and children, with so little regard for the person being hit by them. My life couldn't have felt more normal at home, regardless of how much my appearance made me stand out. Here, in Dolorville, I don't only feel abnormal, I feel like a dartboard, and every insensitivity, every slur, hits the target where it hurts the most.

Often, I sit and imagine myself having the strength and physical ability to speak out, but my unwelcome stutter has me in a chokehold. When Drew and Pop were taken from us, my voice left with them. When they were lowered into the Earth, Mama's voice was buried right along with their bodies. She hasn't spoken a word since the burial service, which we couldn't keep cameras and distant watchers away from. I held her close, felt her shake in my grasp as the caskets lowered. Her cry was hard, but other than sniffles and a few deep breaths, it couldn't be heard. Just felt. It drew more tears out of me, made me hold her even tighter, praying I could carry this misery for her. We weren't just facing unspeakable loss, but the media, paid vultures, were lying about our family, camping outside of our house, and robbing of us of what we needed the most. Privacy. Time.

What wasn't given, we had to take. With just a few bags of clothing and a couple of photos, we fled to Grandma's, a place I never thought I'd consider refuge.

Upon our arrival, our phones beeped, rang, and vibrated back-to-back, so many times, we thought they were malfunctioning. Still in our funeral wear, we sat on Grandma's plaid sofa, and I clicked on a link texted to me, a click that would forever scar us. Just hours after the burials, we, and the rest of the world, learned that Bennett Dickson would not be charged.

My body instantly became a shaking inferno as I listened to the announcement full of disrespectful lies and damaging insinuations. Only seconds after my family's murderer was publicly deemed innocent, Drew's toxicology results, revealing marijuana in his system, were displayed on the screen, followed by my father's face. Large and centered, my hero was accused of criminal trespassing, the location of his bullet-ridden body used as *their* proof.

My heart pounded a beat of rage as Mama rocked slowly, screaming her pain through clenched teeth. On the day they were laid to rest, my family was held responsible for their own murders.

Grandma pulled the phone from my hand. "No more of those lies. Let's keep the devil out of this house." She grabbed her Bible from the coffee table, clutched it, and bowed her head. "God is going to get us through this. You just watch what He does," she stated, tearless, convinced of a belief Mama and I struggled to maintain.

It took everything in us to pry ourselves off the sofa after being read a few scriptures. It felt nearly impossible to put one foot in front of the other and make it to our new rooms, to settle into what was now home, and prepare for all that lay ahead. Life, which still had to go on, and school, which I was still required to finish.

Tragedy led to options, so I chose to finish the final quarter of my junior year online and was set to do the same for my senior year. There was nothing I wanted more than to steer clear of all people, their opinions, unwanted pressure, and maybe achieve the impossible. Heal.

But Mama's sorrows began to eat me alive, and I began to need some form of an escape. I had started to feel so desperate to find more of an existence outside of my grandma's house that I even considered attending school in Dolorville, learning alongside the small town's youth, young fanatics in the making. Gratefully, I didn't have to. Grandma shocked me by sharing information about my only other option, a high school more like the one I previously attended, one that offers a film studies program as a senior elective. It's still hard to believe that Grandma, with her unshakable views, had even searched for schools outside of her physical comfort zone, but I presume after such a great family loss, she felt forced to exercise flexibility for me.

A twenty-minute bus ride, not taken advantage of by any other teens in Dolorville, gave me hope that I was on my way to not just a new school, but to familiarity and healthy distraction. After having what felt like everything ripped from me, even the woman who used to be my mother, I craved school, somewhere to go every day, a course to get lost in, something, anything, to help me hold on to a little piece of myself, to keep what's left of me together.

"Malachi, what do you think?" Mr. Roberts asks, bringing my thoughts back to right here and now, to a classroom I wish I had never stepped foot in.

Silently, I sit, my arms wrapped around my backpack, my eyes on a teacher I haven't learned a thing from. Unsure of what Mr. Roberts wants my opinion on, I shrug as I always do, refusing to stutter publicly in a place where I've already been branded a cursed weirdo.

Grimaces and not-so-low whispers questioning *what* I am, like I'm a thing and not a person, are harsh parts of my new daily experiences. Every day, more pain piles on top of what I moved here with. Here, I face a new level of loneliness, only making me miss my brother more.

Drew was supposed to graduate in early June and should be playing college ball while I should be a senior at the high school I walked into as a freshman. I should be sharing new details about Denise and me with my brother via the daily calls we promised each other and adjusting to what life is like being separated by distance alone. Instead, I'm here, starving for a sense of community, missing the security of friendships, and trying to rebuild myself after being shattered to bits by bullets that tore through me without ever touching me. These unplanned for, unfathomable changes, remain on my mind, have rewritten who I am as a human, and have forever changed how I will walk this earth as a young Black man.

Mr. Roberts steps back to rest against his desk. "We'd love to hear your thoughts, Malachi."

All heads have turned, and all eyes are on me.

"We're discussing the film, *The Bad Seed*," he tells me.

I stare blankly at my teacher through my photophobia glasses and hug the hefty book bag that rests on my legs. Mr. Roberts calls on me every day, though he was present for the meeting my grandmother requested. Grandma had brought everything to light for my new teachers; my stutter, my silence following the murders, and before the meeting concluded, my weekly counseling sessions through the church were noted in my individualized education program. He knows what I've gone through and what I'm still battling, yet he feels the need to call on me daily, to draw unwanted attention to me on a regular basis.

Again, I shrug. I don't move my lips in an even small attempt to speak, against my doctor's advice. With daily practice and intense speech therapy, he's sure my stutter will disappear just as quickly as it returned. Nice thought, but right now, I have it, and struggling in front of a room full of my cruel, immature peers doesn't feel like the best place to work toward speech improvement goals. If anything, I'd be giving them more ammo. If they can so easily link my albinism to evil curses and ghost tales without even using the internet to truly understand what it is, I can't imagine what they'd attribute my stutter to. Likely my intelligence.

Often, I reconsider finishing my senior year at home, though Grandma was right in stating that this school is a lot like my old one. Remodeled, it has multiple sports teams, more class options, and more resources than Dolorville's small town high. But what Grandma failed to look into were the demographics. At one point, they may not have meant as much to me, but undoubtedly, after what I've been through, they do now. To sit in full classrooms where I am the only reason they can be called diverse is triggering. To walk crowded hallways and only spot a few other minorities makes me want to haul ass for the door. But I never do. That'd be quitting, something my father was dead set against, no matter what the situation. Hiding behind a computer screen to escape only a taste of what the rest of the world likely has in store for me would be unacceptable to him. I'm sure he'd view that as an act of weakness, and as difficult as it is for me to show up daily, hiding in Grandma's house would make me feel the same way.

Though fatherless now, I silently apologize to Pop often. He valued my voice, something I don't have anymore. Even in my younger years, no matter how long it would take for me to get out a simple phrase, he'd patiently wait to hear what I had to say, making it clear to me that my words were significant. His lessons have never left me, yet I still remain silent, something he never allowed, something I feel guilty about.

"I loved it," she answers, seated two desks away from me, her preferred seating in the back of the room as well. "I think of *The Bad Seed* as an untouchable classic. Though none of the killings were directly filmed, the acting and storyline were so spot-on, the film didn't need anything extra, not even color."

Mr. Roberts's eyes move to Melody. As she's done before, she answers a question directed at me, pulling all attention her way.

Mr. Roberts nods once at her before briefly looking back at me. I remain tightlipped, my arms still wrapped around my bag, my new comfort when in the presence of a white man.

As Mr. Roberts takes feedback on the classic film from my other classmates, my eyes drift over to Melody, my partner, selected at random, to work with on a short film project. Beneath her seat sits her binder, and as usual, a few books. Atop the pile is a book titled, *White Fragility*. My eyes narrow, trying to read the rest of the words on the cover, but I can't make them out. Since I first took notice of her, she's always had her nose buried in a book or has a few close by. She never carries around novels with dragons, fairies, or teen lovers on the covers, but instead books with titles that make you look at her twice, that make you question, *who is that girl, what has she done, what has she seen or heard in private, what is she trying to rectify?*

My eyes move back up to Melody's face, and she turns toward me as if she can feel my stare. The outer corners of her brown eyes naturally turn downward, making her appear saddened if she's not smiling or expressing another obvious emotion. Down today, her curls are typically pulled up into a high ponytail, revealing a large, salmon colored birthmark that covers most of her neck.

Melody pushes her long brown curls behind her ears as the corners of her mouth rise into a warm smile. She knows not to expect one back and doesn't take it personally. She seems to get why returning the gesture is physically and mentally impossible. Unlike Mr. Roberts and my other schoolmates, Melody allows me to just be. She doesn't appear to be on an obvious mission to embarrass me and has yet to try to force words out of my mouth or push for desired expressions to stretch across my face. So, for now, she's endurable.

Following another of his long-winded rambling sessions, Mr. Roberts asks us to seat ourselves next to our partners to work on the final touches of our short film projects. Eagerly, Melody stands, grabs her books and bag, and heads my way. She places her stack of books on my desk, and as she turns the desk in front of mine to face me, I grab the book atop her pile. As I read over the title, *White Fragility: Why It's So Hard For White People To Talk About Racism,* Melody sits to offer her feedback. "One of the most important pieces I've ever read. There were so many points I hadn't heard before or even thought about deeply. The author really made waves with this book, especially being white and speaking so openly and bluntly about racism."

A cynical chuckle pushes out of me, and I shake my head as I place the book back on top of her others.

"What's wrong? You didn't like it?"

I whip out my phone, our method of communication, and type in my notepad, *Never read it. Don't need to. It's about racism, right? The effects of it on people of color? Well, I think life and experience have taught me all that I need to know.* I hand her my cell.

She nods as her eyes quickly read over my words. "I can understand that. She more so wrote it for us." She points to herself. "By us, I mean white people. Not that Black people shouldn't read it. I'm not saying that at all," she rushes to explain. "I just think she wants to open white eyes, and I hope every white person reads it."

Again, I shake my head and reach out for my phone. I begin typing, *Why does every white person need to read it? Why are her words so eye-opening? Innocent Black lives taken in the middle of the day aren't enough to open white eyes? The tears pouring from the eyes of Black mothers as they stand above their murdered sons and husbands aren't enough? Black children still being deprived of opportunities and fair treatment in their classrooms isn't enough? Black offenders being forced to serve significantly longer sentences than a white person who committed the same crime isn't enough? I pause from typing, take a deep breath, and then resume. That further proves how unimportant Black people still are in this country when viewed through the eyes of white people. Our pain, our losses, our lives aren't taken seriously, aren't eye-opening enough until a white person stands up and says the same thing we've been saying for centuries. Fuck that book,* I type as boiling blood shoots through my veins. *Sounds like race hustling to me.*

As she reads my words, her face flushes. Her eyes move from my phone screen, to the book, and then back again. Without saying a word, she hands me back my phone.

I place it down, then carefully unzip my bag. Before reaching in to pull out my spiral full of our project notes, I quickly glance behind me to ensure Mr. Roberts or one of my peers isn't close enough to see the other contents. Grandma's pastor, my temporary counselor, suggested that I carry around something tangible that makes me feel safe. I'm sure he imagined me toting my bible everywhere, but I carry something else, something that would make everyone else feel the opposite of how it makes me feel. So, I keep it close, but hidden.

"I'm sorry," Melody says, her voice low, filled with shame and a hint of embarrassment. "I just don't believe a white person can claim they aren't racist until they're actively, openly, and regularly practicing antiracism. That's what I'm trying to do. I want to intentionally examine any biases I may have, and I want to…" A tear falls from her right eye, as her words trail off, quickly being replaced by sniffles.

In a panic, I grab my phone and write, *Please, no tears, Melody. If I hurt your feelings, I apologize, but please don't put me in a position to have to explain why you're crying.* I hold the phone out for her to read, and with urgency, she wipes away her tear.

My heart slams against my chest, and I squeeze my backpack the way terrified children squeeze their favorite bears after nightmares. Here I am, incapable of looking at the world the way I used to, and sharing a space with the two most dangerous things in America: a white man and a crying white woman. Her tears are more powerful than anyone's truth. They're enough of a reason to imprison or kill. A white man can in many cases operate as he chooses, hurting whoever he feels is deserving, with little fear of a fair punishment. Me, paler than both, could never truly feel safe in their presence. I know better than anyone what a white man can do without repercussion, and history has shown how destructive the tears of a white woman can be to the Black person who caused them.

"I never cry in public. I didn't mean to make you feel uncomfortable." She forces a smile. "I'm just trying to be the best person I can be in this cold, ugly world and I guess I'm going about that the wrong way."

I shrug before typing, *If her book helps you to be antiracist, I guess I need to stop being so cynical.*

"No, you're right. I'm sure there are many Black authors who have written similar books, and I should check them out."

Another shrug, my backpack held tightly against me. *Maybe you should,* I think to myself, uninterested in carrying on this conversation any longer. It doesn't feel good to know that it takes a white voice to convince other white people that the treatment people of color have and still receive is wrong, but if the end result is more antiracist white people learning alongside me, working within my future career field, and applying to be police officers, many benefit in the end, including me.

My eyes move back to Melody's face. Her sadness, caused by me, pierces my heart. I don't know who I'm becoming. I don't know who was birthed on that deadly Friday afternoon. I can no longer tell if I'm being brutally honest, paranoid, or if I'm just taking my anger out on every white person who crosses my path.

I didn't mean to come across so harshly, I type.

She shakes her head, "No, I appreciate your honesty. I know what you've gone through, Malachi, and I want to know your thoughts. I care about how you feel. How can we be friends if I'm unwilling to hear your truth?"

Friends? She's way ahead of me. I'm just trying to survive in a world that has made it clear to me I'm not truly welcome. New friends, fresh emotional connections, long-lasting bonds—all things I'm not focused on creating right now. I just want respect, to graduate, to pursue my passions, to help my mother find peace again, if possible, and to get the fuck out of Amerikkka; land of inequality and injustice, home of the armed and immoral.

"How about we finish up *Time?*" she suggests, pulling out her laptop.

Time. Our project theme assigned at random. Time. Always depended on, but never reliable. Infinite, but terrifyingly scarce. An opportunity for growth and improvement or stagnation.

Initially, I stared at the word, unsure of where to begin, of what to consider filming that could really make our concept shine. Then, it hit me. I hadn't taken any notes yet, hadn't discussed anything with my partner, but I knew what had come to me in a flash was brilliant, significant, timeless.

With my light bulb still glowing, I began to bullet notes I knew Melody would find moving.

The titles of the books she was always carrying made me sure she'd like to create something uncomfortable and impactful.

I described how I wanted to open the project with an antique grandfather clock centered, in frame. I wanted us to zoom in on the second hand, and the closer the camera moves in, the louder the second hand's ticking would become. Then, I wanted a sudden shatter to cease the ticking, hopefully forcing the eyes of our viewers to widen with curiosity. We'd then zoom out and show the shattering of the clock's glass.

While our theme didn't initially excite me, we agreed it'd at least make a good title. The title would fade in atop the shattered glass, upright in white lettering and then reflected upside down in black.

My hand moved enthusiastically, note-taking sloppily, and Melody read as I wrote. I wanted to take more of a documentary approach, maybe including interviews, but I changed my mind as I decided against audio. I wanted the power of the images and muted clips to sound off in the minds of our viewers, for the emotion to translate, similarly to how silent films once had to bear the burden of telling an interesting story without sound.

Now, only a couple of weeks from presentation day, with most of the film put together, we've found ourselves stuck on the ending. Unfortunately, there were countless images and short videos for us to choose from to show the similarities between past and modern-day lynchings. We had our pick of images showing slaves in chains and Black men in cuffs. There were countless photos and videos of unarmed Black victims being beaten or gunned down by police officers.

We didn't have to dig deep to find photos of past and present epidemics. From the suicides of gay men, to sexual assaults, to homelessness, to mass shootings, to past and current civil rights movements, we found images and short videos about so many things that should've never existed, and even worse, still do today. With an overwhelming amount of relevant material to include, we've been stuck, beating our heads against the wall, trying to bring something to a close that hasn't actually concluded.

With no winning ideas for a proper ending, I mentally go through what we've already put together, hoping for a creative lightning bolt to strike. Through photos of crying mothers, distraught children wearing their deceased father's faces on their shirts, wide shots of mass graves, terrified students escaping school shootings, and shivering homeless people sleeping under bridges, we plan to evoke emotion in our viewers.

Something so powerful can't be wrapped carelessly, and I refuse to count on the beginning and middle to deliver the message. My art has to be shown in its most complete form, make the right statements, move those who watch, and stand one of life's most difficult tests. Time.

"I had a thought about the ending," Melody interjects. "I don't know how you're going to feel about it. I...I..." Her voice shakes. "I don't want to step on your toes, but I think it could truly make our project even more profound."

I tilt my head, eyeing her intently.

"I did a little research," she says, her eyes moving as quickly as her fingers across the keyboard. "I found some photos, some interviews, and I knew this would be powerful because it's so recent and so close to all of us."

I slouch back in my seat, still hugging my bag, my phone clenched in my right hand.

She shifts in her seat before clearing her throat. "If you're open to it, I promise to let you decide how you want to add it."

My eyes remain on her, though hers remain fixed on her laptop screen.

"I won't push you to do more than you're comfortable with," she says.

I'm already uncomfortable, and I don't know what the idea is yet. No one beats around the bush this much about something inoffensive. *Come on, Melody. Come on out with the bullshit.*

With my eyes on her, still leaned back in my seat, she spins her laptop around for me to see. On her screen is an article titled, *Half A Family Gunned*

Down; One Spared. Enlarged and centered, beneath the title, sits a photo of Andrew, Pop, Rocko, and me. Mama hasn't been included at all.

I don't read past the title. I turn away, breathe through the anger, try to cool myself as heatwaves move through me.

"I know that I'll never fully understand how painful your experience was, but I think it goes to show how much ugliness still exists in this world and how much work still needs to be done," she says softly.

I don't make eye contact with Melody. Instead, I look up at the large clock and scoff at the time. Thirty minutes left in this room. Thirty more minutes to sit and stew in this growing, thick energy with someone no longer tolerable.

"I know the details differ from article to article, and nobody will ever know the full story except for those who were there, but I'm sure your father and brother were nothing like they were described."

My eyes shoot to hers.

"They were killed because of their race, but you were..." Her voice fades, and I so badly want to fill the uncomfortable silence between us.

I was what? I was what? Say it. Speak the nonsense so many journalists have printed. Believe the foolishness social media trolls have shared repeatedly.

56

"I know your family is Black. I mean, African American," she says quickly. "Unfortunately, their skin made them targets for racists. But you," She brushes her hand over her curls. "You were born without their complexion, and because you were born with white skin, you were spared."

My heart hammers against my chest. Moisture fills my pits. Sweat slowly trickles down my back.

"I think sharing why you're still here and still alive would be the perfect way to wrap. You're our peer and classmate. That's such a personal ending. It'd be unforgettable."

Hands shaking, sweat breaking out all over me, I release my firm hold on my backpack and begin to type. *Learn to ask questions because you have it all wrong. I wasn't spared because I'm albino. I was spared, if that's what you want to call it, because I was home with my mother. Had I been there, I'd have just been another dead body on his lawn.* I pause, draw a deep breath, and continue. *Albinism is an inherited disorder. I may lack pigment, but I have a race. It's the same as my father's and brother's. It's the reason the triggerman treated me just as shitty as he did my family when he'd see me walking. This skin doesn't protect me. My color doesn't hide what I still am. And what I am, I'm proud of.*

I hold the phone out for her to grab. As her eyes move across my words, I stare at my hands. With a glance, I look over at Melody's hands and then gaze back at my skin, skin whiter than hers. Since I've been here, I've been gossiped about, feared for possibly being cursed, called a white Black man, evil, contagious, you name it. But the worse thing I've been called is lucky. Whispers of being *the lucky one* because of the skin I'm in disgusts me. The whispers make me want to revisit my days of intense Jiu Jitsu training and choke the whisperers until they can't speak my name again, until they're incapable of making any more outlandish assumptions about me and my family.

Melody gently lies the phone face down on my desk. With a lowered head, she quietly says, "I'm so sorry. The last thing I ever wanted to do was offend you or come across as ignorant. I mean, maybe I am." She shrugs. "I'm sure I am about a lot of things, but I'm trying to learn because I want to be better than others who simply choose to hide behind their privilege, only looking at these tragedies from the outside, feeling as though it's not their problem to get involved in. This is a countrywide issue, and I want to be a part of the change. I want to make a difference."

I don't pick up my phone, don't begin to type a response to what she's just shared. I grip my bag and think about our project; its ending. I think about all the women and men of color that I deeply admire. Just the sight of their faces, the reading of their names, inspires me and makes me feel like I can do anything. The ending should feature them, the familiar faces of powerful individuals so many of us, no matter what race, respect and hold in high regard.

That's our ending, I realize immediately. Following a display of so many well-known and much-loved icons, we can film fired bullets up close, and in slow motion, make them move back into barrels. Bodycam videos will be played in reverse, putting life back into the bodies of those gunned down. As the reversals play, a transparent clock will spin counterclockwise, until the fade-in of our final screen.

The final screen will display as many innocent victims as we can fit, and we'll leave our viewers with these words to read; *They could've been the next Black president, the next great inventor, the one to discover the cure for cancer or Alzheimer's. They were full of possibilities and could've made monumental impacts that could've changed the lives of millions, had they just been given the time.*

SURVIVORS

I, the only one to get off at my stop, exit the school bus and begin my daily walk toward Grandma's. Though the walk is short, strolling through Dolorville feels like time-traveling. We used to joke about this place being the town that time forgot, and I was relieved to not live here, but *here* is where I ended up, residing where I'm unwelcome.

Hands in my pockets, I stroll past small, dated, brick-front stores and the same faces I see every day, each one saddened or disgusted at the sight of me. With my headphones in, welcoming no conversation or scripture readings, I move along hoping I won't have to hear one more person tell me they're going to pray for my mother and grandmother. If you're going to pray for them, just do it. I don't need to be told and deliberately excluded. No speech necessary.

I come upon the local pharmacy, the only one in Dolorville, which I struggle to believe carries enough prescriptions to cover even the most common ailments. The tiny storefront's window is lined with faux yellow mums and covered in decals beginning to peel along their edges. Mr. Wallace, the pharmacist, smirks as he waves through the window. I raise my hand half-heartedly as I continue on, refusing to pretend that I like him even a little.

My first time crossing paths with Mr. Wallace after moving to town, I was picking up toiletries for Mama. As I was checking out, he stared studiously, barely looking at the items as he scanned them. His prying eyes remained on me up until the final item was bagged. Before reading my total, his lips finally parted, and he asked, "What's going on with you? Is this one of those Michael Jackson situations? I've heard about people like you, who mess up their bodies, trying not to stay Black." I didn't answer him, didn't type how much of an ill-informed asshole he was, never even waited for a total. I tossed my twenty on the counter and snatched my bag, only to be slapped by my grandmother upon entering her house.

The sting of her palm across one cheek, followed by a jolt of pain from a back-hand across the other, shocked the breath right out of me. Disrespect to an elder isn't tolerated, and I was never given the opportunity to explain my side. His phone call beat me home, and all my grandmother needed to hear was that I threw money at him and walked off rudely.

Grandma disciplined me, something my mother would never be okay with, but wasn't made aware of. Without my mother's knowledge, she threatened even harsher punishments should I ever disrespect another elder again. Now, Mr. Wallace waves arrogantly, and to prevent tension in my new home, I return the gesture Grandma wants versus the one he deserves.

Almost at the corner, the pharmacy now behind me, I squint behind my glasses, trying to pull in a clearer image of who has no business being in Dolorville. I slow my pace and narrow my eyes even more as my stomach twists. Moving slowly, but closer toward her, coolness washes over me in a shower of relief. I'm not looking at Denise.

Denise, my first love, the only girlfriend I've ever had, was someone I once couldn't imagine getting through a full day without talking to. What was considered puppy love to most couldn't have felt more real to us. Or so I thought.

Following the shootings, Denise was supportive, texting me throughout the day, and considerate enough to refrain from asking inappropriate questions or pushing the subject, which I wasn't ready to fully discuss.

I had felt proud to call her mine, to have her support, though I wasn't comfortable stuttering through phone conversations with her. The person I thought was an understanding girlfriend turned out to be an attention-needing media whore. Denise was giving statements to the news outlets and making comments she didn't have enough information to make. She was also reciting outright lies, stating that she was on the phone with me when shots rang out and declaring that she and Andrew had become best friends after we began dating. She tied herself so closely to my brother that, had I not known him better, I'd question his loyalty. But I knew Drew. I watched their respectable interactions, and they weren't any closer than I was to Andrew's girl. Denise just wanted to be seen. Unfortunately, I saw her, and what I saw, I didn't respect or want.

While Denise disappointed me in a way I never saw coming, she will forever remain in my heart as my first love and the reason I stayed home that Friday. Had I not been so anxious to vent to her, to hear her laugh followed by that adorable snort, and to make plans for our next date, I'd have accepted Pop's invitation and taken that walk. The last walk of my life.

As I move toward who I had initially thought was someone I'd never want to see again, the sudden realization of who is standing there makes my feet feel planted, frozen. I'm uncertain of the right words to say, if they even exist, if I'll even be able to get them out.

She turns. Her jet-black mane is thick, wild, blowing in the crisp fall breeze. Her large, deep-set eyes are as dark and rich as her silky complexion.

Our eyes meet, and years dissolve, immediately blown away with the fallen leaves. I feel like a twelve-year-old again, heart beating wildly at the sight of her, just like it used to when we'd visit for Thanksgiving and see her growth after a full year.

Visiting Grandma wasn't the most exciting thing to do as a child, but not every kid in town was a Sunday school goody two shoes. There was also Nikki. Both Andrew and I had a crush on her, and those crushes only grew more serious as the years passed and her body thickened.

Nikki was always the bluntest, the funniest, and the most fearless, making it impossible to not notice her and want to be her friend.

I force my feet to move as she steps toward me. Neither of us smiles as we close the space between us. Without words spoken, Nikki pulls me into a firm embrace.

"I'm so sorry about Andrew and your pop. So, so, sorry," she whispers.

I hold her tight. "S-s-s..." I pause, try again. "S-s-s..." My mouth trembles as I try to offer my own condolences to her, sadly not the only broken heart in this hug. Nikki recently lost someone who meant the world to her too. Joseph, her best friend, gay, bullied, and isolated in this cult-like place. He was the pastor's son, and from what I remember about our interactions, was kind and fairly shy. He was nationwide news as well, and according to my grandmother, the only reason *the devil* came to her town.

The story was, Joseph was shot in his home by an older lover he met online. The day prior to the start of the trial, Joseph hanged himself in his aunt's home, leaving behind a letter that stated he saw who attempted to take his life, and it wasn't the man accused.

It was wild for us to see the names and faces of people we knew trending on social media and being spoken about by major news outlets. Joseph and I didn't interact as much as Nikki and I did during our visits, but I have no bad memories with him. It seemed pretty obvious to Pop that Joseph was gay. He caught on before Andrew and I did. Maybe because we couldn't think or see past Nikki. But once Pop realized it, he brought it to our attention and demanded that we continue to treat him with respect, though treating him otherwise had never crossed our minds. Pop threatened to knock the shit out of us if he were to ever hear of us bullying Joseph. He had always taught us to meet people where they are and give them a chance with our eyes wide open. In front of my grandmother, who couldn't and still can't discuss the topic without cringing and praying, Pop explained that homosexuality is not airborne and stated that playing ball with Joseph wasn't going to make us gay, but ultimately better men. He told us to treat Joseph like we would any other kid, and we did.

"S-s-s…" I release a frustrated, deep sigh. *Fuck!* I want to tell her how sorry I am that she lost her best friend. I want her to hear those words come from me. I don't want to type them. I want to say them.

"It's okay," she says as our arms fall from around each other. "I know you are."

My eyes look into hers. Where fire and determination used to live, sadness now resides.

I look away as tears build. Nikki was the one who always said the unexpected, who always accepted you no matter how different you were, and who would kick the shit out you if you were to speak ill of Joseph in her presence. But here in front of me, I see defeat. I see damage. I see what I see when I look at my mother.

Mama used to say that Nikki is a lot like her. Both were raised here, stuck here throughout their childhoods, but something in them just couldn't adopt the extreme principles that recycle here. Nikki, like Mama, is love. They're walking hearts, open and ready to pour into anyone, whether that person is gay, a churchgoer, an atheist, or convinced they're an alien. They're two of the strongest females I know, both beaten and broken down by the ugliness of their worlds.

"How's Ms. Deborah?"

I shake my head disappointedly as I have to pull out my phone. I type, *She's in pieces. She hasn't spoken a word since the burial.*

Mama isn't only inconsolably silent, but her body radiates heat. Not because she's feverish, but because she's enraged from her moment of waking until the moment her pills force her to meet the sandman. Mama isn't just a grieving mother and widow, but a coward to the world who has no interest in understanding her immeasurable pain. Everybody wants her statement, her eye-witness testimony, her words of disappointment regarding the lack of charges. Everybody wants to see her fight. The world wants her out in the streets, publicly, on the front lines. No one realizes she is fighting. She's fighting to stay alive, to find the confidence to take every next breath, which I'm only convinced she takes because I'm here, still in need of a parent.

"I can't imagine her pain," Nikki says, after reading my words. "I wanted to pay my respects, but after JJ…" A tear falls, and she wipes it away with her sweatshirt sleeve. "Do you know that son of a bitch didn't even have a funeral for his own son? Some pastor." She shakes her head. Her face twists in disgust. "I guess suicidal gay teens aren't deserving of proper homegoing services. I guess their lives aren't worth anything in the eyes of church folks."

My head drops in disbelief. Grandma was under the impression the services were private and for the immediate family only. To not have a service for your own child is a new level of low, and this is the man my grandmother expects to provide me with life-changing counseling.

"I literally hate that man, Malachi. I'm convinced he's the one Joseph was talking about in his suicide letter. He shot his own son, and I'm not going to let him get away with this shit. He threw my best friend in the ground and expected everyone to just forget about him. Well, I'll always remember him, and I'm going to keep rubbing him in everyone's faces."

My eyes widen at her words and then slowly move down to her t-shirt, which I'm just now taking notice of. In bold, rainbow text, all caps, the words say, JUSTICE FOR JOSEPH. Beneath those words is his face. His smile impales my heart. I knew him. I attended a few Sunday School classes with him. We played together. He was a good person, a human in his own lane, on his own journey, beaten down in every way for just being himself.

A tear escapes me as well, and Nikki wipes it from my cheek. Joseph deserved so much more. He deserved to live his truth without persecution, just as my family deserved to be able to safely walk down the street as Black men.

"I've copied hundreds of pictures of Joseph. I've taped them to the church walls, folded them inside the Bibles and hymn books. I'm not letting these fucking devils forget what they did to him. Their words and their treatment played a role in his ending, and it's my duty to make sure they never forget what they did."

I look at Nikki. I listen as she describes how she's fighting for her friend, watch as the fire reignites in her eyes as she speaks. Though I know Nikki is doing this for Joseph, this is also probably the only way she feels she can grieve and still exist here. This is how she gets through the day, how she survives after such a great loss.

"I should be in fucking college right now, but I can't leave him yet. I can't leave him here, in Hell, nobody visiting his grave but me."

I pull Nikki close and wrap my arms around her again. I hold her tightly, realizing that it doesn't matter where you live. Hate exists everywhere. It's inescapable.

Nikki cries into my jacket. "I know why you guys came here. Joseph and I wanted to leave, to move to a city together, to escape the homophobia and find normalcy. Y'all came to escape racism and the media. But you know what, Malachi? You know what?" She cries harder, forcing more tears out of me. "There's nowhere to fucking go. You leave one problem just to find another."

Nikki and I hold each other, crying on the sidewalk, our tears carried away in the strengthening breeze, but our pain still heavy and darkening within us.

I don't look around, but I'm sure passersby are taking note of our extended embrace, marking it in their minds as sinful, and preparing to share it with our folks. I don't let her go. Not yet. Not when I know no one in this town will let her truly grieve her loss.

Briefly, I release her and type, *Next time you plan to visit his grave, let me know. I'd like to pay my respects.* I wrap one arm back around her, and with my other hand, hold my phone screen only inches from her face.

Her arms tighten around me. "I'd appreciate having you there. Someone else who cares about him, you know? He'd appreciate that too."

Isolated in life, practically discarded after his death, and forgotten as if he were a stranger met in passing, Joseph lies alone in a cemetery within walking distance of those he grew up with and the parents he was raised by. While I believe souls leave our bodies in death, the lack of visitors to his grave is indicative of how little his life was valued by those who are now my neighbors. The thought stabs through the middle of me, making me twitch.

Nikki pulls back. "You okay?"

Far from it. I'm fucking disgusted.

She nods as though she can hear my thoughts. "I'm glad you guys found a place to catch your breath, but you're too good for this town, Malachi. Leave before they run you out or break you down."

Run me out. Break me down. What's the difference? I don't type a response to her statement. Dolorville, a godforsaken place, may have the ability to hurt me, to play darts with what's left of my heart, but after what I've been through, after what I've lost, I can't be shattered. I already am. I can't be run out. I've already run.

I look over Nikki's face. I want to encourage her to take her own advice, to leave, to never return, but after what she's explained to me, I decide not to. She's fighting in the only way she knows how. This fight isn't just for Joseph, but for her healing as well. I'm inclined to believe it makes the heartbreak more bearable for her. It's how she's surviving a pain that likely eats away at her during all of her still moments. It's a pain I know all too well. It's a pain I pour into my film projects, a pain I don't think I could survive if I didn't fill my time.

Nikki and I exchange numbers before hugging once more. Keen on sneaking into the church to leave more copies of Joseph's face, she rushes off. I watch as she dashes away, inspired and yet fearful of the disappointment she's likely to face when her fight doesn't bring her the satisfaction she so desperately needs. When they lock her out of the church, when years pass and Joseph's father is still standing behind his pulpit earning looks of admiration from his entire community, how will Nikki cope? Will she feel as though she fought a losing battle? Will she rest knowing she did all she could?

I arrive at Grandma's, my thoughts cycling between Nikki, my murdered loved ones, my mother's wellbeing, and my project. I enter, closing the door gently. Loud bangs, slammed doors, and unexpected popping sounds all trigger Mama, especially if I'm not within her line of sight.

I slowly push her already cracked bedroom door open. On her side, she lies silently, cuddling a framed photo of our once whole family. On her bedside table, which still holds her music box and childhood Bible, sits a full glass of water. It's impossible to know whether she refilled the glass, but my gut tells me this is the glass I placed there for her this morning.

Carefully, I place my hefty backpack on the floor, lean in, and kiss my mother's face. Cheeks that used to glow radiantly are now dry with scaly patches. Eyes that happiness used to shine through appear darker and devoid of joy and hope.

I run my hand across her thick, unkempt hair before reaching over for her glass of water. Mama responds by slowly pushing herself into an upright position.

I take notice of her shaky hands. I want to take them both in mine, hold them, help her find the strength that I, too, am seeking, but her body is craving something, likely hydration and nutrition.

Mama used to be health-obsessed. She was the owner of a successful, all-natural skincare line that averaged 4.8 stars. She encouraged us to repeat daily affirmations to keep our subconscious minds strong and filled with positivity. She meditated daily, without fail. Now, Mama is a mute, doesn't post affirmations around our common spaces, doesn't practice self-care anymore, barely eats, and spends a majority of her time in bed.

I sit before holding the glass to her lips, encouraging her to take small swallows of what her body is in desperate need of. I look over her face, her thinner and sunken-in cheeks. I look at the darkness that's made a home under her eyes. I take notice of the dryness of her lips that's led to cracking. Mama is trying so hard, trying with the little she has left to keep going, but day by day, I notice she's slipping away more and more. Pain that was expected to subside hasn't, not even slightly. A framed photo that used to sit on her bedside table now lies on the pillow beside her. She cuddles it, keeps it close to her heart, cries with it in her arms. What we were told would ultimately fade seems to grow.

This grief isn't comparable to anything we've felt before. When Grandpa died due to complications from diabetes, pain stormed in, but it didn't last. It wasn't hurt that stayed behind to haunt us, but acceptance that took up permanent residence inside of our hearts. When Drew and I lost two friends in a car wreck, we were cut deep, but were able to recover. This heartbreak, this trauma, it's debilitating, especially in quiet moments. It never leaves us. It's there, something I've worked hard to distract myself from, but haven't learned how to silence and heal from. When silence arrives, the gunshots fire, the smell of death fills the space I'm in, heartache stabs me repeatedly, and a battle I often doubt I will survive begins. My stomach pangs rob me of an appetite, sometimes for an entire day, leading to shaking spells and incurable headaches. The unwanted images of blood pouring from their bodies tases me, sending high voltages of pain throughout my body, making it hard for me to do the simplest tasks, like taking steps, even standing. Then the deluge of tears begins, nearly drowning me, making breathing feel like an impossibility. School, creating my projects, and caring for Mama forces my mind to focus on other things. But Mama, she can't bring herself to move past that day. What I can temporarily distract myself from, Mama experiences all day, multiple times a day. It's nearly crippled her.

Mama pulls back from the glass, about a third consumed. I want to push her to drink more, but I set the glass down to catch the tear rolling down her face. I want to pull out my phone and tell her it'll be okay, but I don't want to accidentally lie because I don't know that it will be. I want to tell her I bumped into Nikki, someone she's always adored and spoke highly of, but I don't want to have to tell her the things Nikki shared with me about Joseph. Mama's crushed enough. I don't need anything else burying her deeper into a pit of depression and hopelessness.

I open my arms, and lazily, Mama falls forward in between them. I inch over and hug her tightly. I do what she wishes my father were here to do, what she wishes Andrew could still do, and even her big boy, Rocko. I comfort her. I pour my love into her, all the love I have left to give.

Her flesh feels hot. Her body trembles. Her sobs nearly bring out some of my own, but I try to avoid that. I don't want to spend the rest of my day crying and being cut repeatedly by the sharpness of merciless grief.

I carefully pull back from Mama, holding onto her shaky arms, ensuring she doesn't fall over. I wipe away freshly fallen tears from beneath both eyes and kiss her warm forehead. As she watches, I rise to my feet and grab her robe.

With her bathrobe draped over my shoulder, we take slow steps toward the small, outdated bathroom at the end of the hall. I release one of her unsteady hands to twist the tacky, faux crystal doorknob, opening up the door for Mama to enter. I never pull the door closed for her. I always wait for her to close it, so it never feels as though I'm leaving her.

Though Mama uses the shower stool I ordered her, I can't bring myself to move from the other side of the closed door as she showers. She can appear so fragile, and I want to be close in case she falls, in case she needs me.

I lean against the wall opposite the bathroom door as she takes her time and moves about the small space. When I hear the shower turn on, I hurry to her bedroom to grab my weighty backpack from the floor. In seconds, I return.

Sitting with my back against the wall, I pull out the permission slip Mr. Roberts gave out at the end of class, inviting film studies students to visit an old theater. About thirty minutes away from the school, tucked in another small town, the building is currently owned, but has not been rehabbed. Described by Mr. Roberts as a one-of-a-kind viewing experience, he decided it'd be there that we present our short film projects, in the evening, movie-premiere style.

Looking forward to anything seemed impossible just hours earlier, but this I am. An evening trip, where I'll get to debut my film project is not something I could imagine missing. Not unless Grandma has an unmissable church event that evening, in which case, I'll stay with Mama.

Most relentless after the sun kisses us goodbye for the day, Mama's struggles brutalize her throughout the evenings, up until medication hour. Her being alone after dark, submerged in her own tears, isn't something I'd ever allow. I want to attend, but I'll pass up this trip for my mama. He may no longer be here, but I still follow Pop's teachings to protect Mama first until the day I have a wife to protect.

I keep the permission slip in hand as my eyes fall to my opened backpack, something I need to clutch almost the entire school day. Inside the bag I hold to feel safe lies the loaded Glock 9mm my Pop taught my brother and me how to use safely in case of a home invasion.

Beginning the night of the shooting, I needed our family protection tucked underneath my pillow to even remain put. What I thought I'd eventually be okay without, I can't seem to leave behind when facing a mixed environment. It's the only thing that makes me feel protected, the only thing that makes me feel like I have a fighting chance the next time I encounter another Bennett infecting the world.

I zip my bag, hide away my comfort item, and place my backpack in between my legs. I let my head rest against the wood paneling as the saddest sounds escape the bathroom. Mama's weeping, which is louder than the water hitting the tub's floor.

Alone on her side of the door, and me sitting outside of it, our tears fall. Not temporary tears, but tears we'll be crying for the rest of our lives. We share this tragedy, but our hurt isn't identical. Our inner battles aren't the same, though caused by the same bullets. Still, we're both fighting, unsure of whether or not we're in an emotional battle that'll end in our victory, unsure of whether or not we'll ever rediscover the ability to get through a day without breaking down.

For now, we remain on a horrific rollercoaster ride, unbuckled, never knowing what the next minute holds and if we're just seconds from another loop of incapacitating emotion. We're constantly trying to remember what strength is, desperately missing our taken three, and remain slaves to our recollections of that bloody Friday.

Imbalanced, irreparably broken, and endlessly trying best describe us now. Every second of our day, we're consciously trying to make it to the next. There isn't a moment we aren't putting forth effort, constantly forcing ourselves to go on. We're not living as we may appear to be. We're surviving.

FATE

How could we possibly be the masters of something we have no control of choosing? Isn't fate defined as something beyond one's control, something determined by a supernatural power? The idea that I could possibly master something that's already designed to go a certain way doesn't make me feel hopeful, but instead angry with the individual trying to convince me of such a strange concept.

I sit in the front pew, my arms folded across my chest, my backpack at Grandma's, not needed at my side in Dolorville. Racism doesn't live here. Just ignorance.

"Are you listening to me?" he asks loudly, like a father to their young child who's playing when they should be paying attention.

I nod slowly, my response truthful. I'm listening to Grandma's beloved pastor speak, but I refuse to take anything this hateful narcissist says to heart.

"I know talking isn't your thing, but you could nod, give me a thumbs up, clap if need be, without me having to ask you to."

I immediately notice that every suggested response would communicate my approval of the things he's saying. He didn't suggest that I shake my head or give him a thumbs down. That's because he doesn't expect or accept a difference of opinion, though he's contradicted himself quite a bit in the short time he's been talking *at* me, versus to me. In the same breath, he told me my future is in God's hands and His plan for me will unfold the way it's meant to. Then, he shouted that I'm the master of my fate and my response to my trauma will determine how I end up. *Will it? Does it matter what I do if the plan has already been determined for me?* Based on that notion, Drew, my father, and Rocko were all fated to be gruesomely murdered on that scarring Friday for no other reason than it being God's plan. If that's the case, no wonder I'm struggling to hold on to my faith.

"As I've mentioned during our other counseling sessions, your communication struggles may not be as out of your control as you think. Maybe you're getting something out of having a stutter. Maybe your so-called stutter offers you a benefit." His eyes remain on me as he arrogantly cocks his head. "Maybe that's why you aren't actively working on speaking out loud. Having this issue could be getting you special attention or getting you out of conversations you don't want to have."

He remains silent for a moment as though he expects me to suddenly speak as fluidly as he believes I secretly can.

"This is your life, Malachi. Take your fate into your own hands."

I begin to type his words for him to read. *I can't take it into my own hands. It's in God's hands, remember?*

With my phone held out, he leans forward to read my words, grunting irritably once done. "You know, maybe instead of mocking me, you could show some gratitude for me counseling you week after week. You aren't a part of my congregation. Your mother doesn't attend service. I'm here to show you a kindness."

How kind of you to keep insinuating that my stutter isn't real. How kind of you to show no compassion for my mother who suffers every second of every day. My grandmother practically worships this man who has yet to even visit her daughter. He wants everyone in this church, filling these pews, clapping, fainting, and deifying him. Us silent folks, those who are being held hostage by misery, are met with arrogance and ugly insinuations because we can't give him what he needs. Adoration. Praise.

Back at what used to be home, we weren't consistent church-goers, but our old pastor showed up at the funeral, far from angered that he wasn't asked to be a part of it. Within the sympathy card he handed us was a hefty check, some of the money from him and his wife, the rest collected from his congregation. He consistently emails us to check in and send us scriptures, though I've let him know why Mama's not responding and has yet to cash the check. Our small financial contributions and inconsistent attendance never deterred him from showing us love and compassion, and my appearance has never created awkwardness between us. His heart and arms have remained open, and that's what my parents have raised me to believe Christianity is. I don't know what this town's religion is, though I know what they want it to be.

"Maybe instead of mocking the Lord and His plan for you, you could take a moment to reflect on why you were spared."

Spared. I fucking despise that word. It makes me sound as though I was the fortunate one, like they were chosen and I wasn't, like living without my loved ones and watching my mother deteriorate is some kind of a prize.

"I bet when you were old enough to recognize your differences, you thought you were weird. Maybe you even wished to look like everyone else. But take a minute and think about how being different has benefited you. How much of a blessing is it that your appearance, what may have felt like a disadvantage at times, is what ultimately prevented you from being targeted?"

I scoff loudly, unworried about the disrespect I'm sure will be reported back to my grandmother. I'll take the slap. The sting won't last long. What I won't do, physically can't do, is sit calmly as foolish people speak matter-of-factly on something they're clueless about. I physically don't match my relatives. I am paler than most white people. Truths, but one big one, and to me, the most important one, is often left unspoken. I am an albino, something I've grown to accept and be proud of, but I am not without race. I'm without color. I'm still and always will be Black.

"I'm going to let that slide," he says, doing me no favors. I know Grandma will hear *his* truths about this session.

I refuse to give him a smile, a nod, or any other bullshit version of an undeserving *thank you*. I will not applaud an insult or encourage him to preach more of his nonsense. While I've been able to maintain my cool throughout our other sessions, his comment about being spared made it impossible to not react.

Dolorville's beloved pastor's eyes darken with hate, and his dark brows raise at their outer corners, changing the entire look of his face. My heartbeat begins to gallop so rapidly, so loudly, I question if he can hear it. Heat covers me, and I shift in my seat.

My stomach flips as the bright building, built to be a place of love, suddenly feels heavy, unbreathable, stifling.

I blink rapidly. My eyes move to the large cross centered at the head of the updated church, then back to his eyes of fury. All it took was one audible form of disapproval for his mask to fall off.

I stand, wanting to get out of here as quickly as humanly possible. I've spent enough time in this house of God being preached to by the devil.

Immediately, my mind goes back to Nikki, to her accusations that I didn't doubt, but can now more easily believe while in his presence.

"Sit back down," he orders.

I don't. I've been around evil, looked it right in the eyes within an hour of seeing the carnage it can create. But this is a different kind of evil, a more dangerous one, empowered by every service he holds. Every applause strengthens him. He's trusted and believed the moment he opens his mouth. He's capable of doing just about anything he wants and most times will likely go unquestioned, all because he's believed to be a man of the cloth.

I turn my back on the hateful man, on eyes filled with darkness that say all I need to know. I turn away from who I refuse to ever interact with again once I leave this session.

I slowly head for the church's double doors but pause after passing only a few pews. Lying on the end of an unoccupied wooden bench is a Bible lying face up. I reach down and grab it. Slowly, I open it, not in search of a scripture, but of a photo. And here it is. Folded inside, near the middle of the holy book, is Joseph's face. So young, full of life unlived, the victim of a fate his father refuses to mention. With his photo in hand, I begin typing a message in my notepad. *Fate sounds like something you believe God has full control over, yet you somehow believe I can alter my own. Maybe we'd connect better if I could relate to you. You've suffered a great loss too. Your son committed suicide. From what I hear, he was an outcast for being gay. I personally don't have anything against gay people, but from what I hear, you do. Speaking of fate, was it God's plan for you to have a gay son, and if so, how can his homosexuality be wrong? If it's you who has control of your fate, did you want a gay son?*

I turn around with Joseph's photo, Nikki's weapon against Dolorville's hateful residents still in my hand. I move toward the pastor, a father I wouldn't wish on any child. Standing in front of him once again, I hold my phone out for him to read.

As his eyes pull in my words, his brows furrow. Patiently, I stand as evil has to face itself, its truths. He never admits to being wrong because in his warped reality, he isn't. So, if what he's been stating to me are facts, they must apply to him as well.

His nostrils flare, the outer ends of his brows rise again as his eyes, black holes, slowly leave the screen and find mine.

His face appears more sinister than it did before, but I don't look away. With the flick of my wrist, I flip open the creased photo of Joseph and reveal it before his father's face.

He never looks at it, doesn't show care, doesn't utter a response to my words.

Nostrils still widened, he bites down on his bottom lip and sighs loudly. "Exit this blessed place, and take that trash with you."

Trash. His son. His deceased son, who must've been in such unbearable pain to feel like ending his own life was his only option.

I shake my head. *Shame on this beast.* I don't know what's in store for him, but based on what I've seen, fate's endings seem unjust and much harsher than one could ever deserve. If my loving family's fate was to be gunned down in broad daylight by a racist, and Joseph's was to live a life so painful that hanging himself was his only escape, something vile and even more dreadful must be awaiting this demon. Something hard to hear, too terrifying to imagine, too sick to even describe, has to be the last stop of his life's journey, and I'm not ashamed to admit that I can't wait to see what that merciless fate will be.

DOLORVILLE

Side by side, on our knees, our heads hang. I shiver as fallen leaves blow by, one landing on his flat headstone; simple, gray, with only his name and his years of birth and death. There are no sentiments and no flowers other than ones we brought. I've visited graves before, but this one feels particularly empty.

I peek over at Nikki as she rocks back and forth, head lowered, grief-stricken, fuming inside. I slide my hand over and grab hers. I wish I could take her pain away, or at least lessen it, but how can one broken heart heal another?

Nikki and I have been texting for almost two weeks now, often sharing walks and trying to carry out normal conversations, but our lives are drenched in sorrow. She says she's willing to listen to whatever I need to get off my chest, but drowning her in my pain when she's sinking in her own isn't my idea of a fair friendship.

I've given her the undetailed version of what I go through living here and attending my new high school, which immediately reminded her of what Joseph used to go through on a daily basis. The whispers, the looks, the rumors, the false news, the disrespectful questions, ate Joseph alive, but not quickly. Slowly. Small bites.

I can understand how. Words cut. The harsher they are, the more unforgettable they become. They leave you bleeding internally. They linger, just to creep in inconveniently and peel back the scab that took forever to form. Insults you wish were powerless follow you like a shadow. Some days they're not on the forefront of your mind, not an obvious thought, more of a hovering cloud, controlling your energy. Other days, you can hear the words exactly as they were spit in your face, can feel yourself shudder and tear up at the ugliness of them. Words—they create breaks no cast or surgery can fix.

After being compared to Joseph, I decided not to share one more word about my new struggles, and instead focused on my short film. Nikki was Joseph's only support, his only listening ear. I can't imagine the emotional burden he unintentionally placed on her. I refuse to add to what she may not realize she's still carrying.

I squeeze her hand, my eyes on Joseph's name, my mind drifting to my brother, on how different life was when he was still here, when we were inseparable, always holding hands without having to touch. I wasn't ridiculed, bad-mouthed, made to feel like a pariah. I felt like him, not just well-known, but loved and accepted. I felt so included that at times, I forgot how different I looked. It was a blessing, and one I didn't take for granted. It's what inspired me to support other albinos online. I didn't have years of bullying to unpack and heal from, so I was able to be a shoulder for those who were forced to digest discriminatory slurs on a daily basis. Now, living in a hell that was once unfamiliar to me, I'm in need of a shoulder of my own, and as bad as Nikki believes she can be that for me, her pieces need glue too.

Nikki weeps. One of her trembling, sweaty hands is gripped inside mine, the other rests on Joseph's headstone. I can feel her longing, her desperation. She'd do anything for him to still be here, just as I would to hug Pop once more, to lie in the dark making college plans with Drew just one last time. The holes that exist within our hearts can't be filled. We will never be free of our suffering, though we've been told repeatedly that the days will get easier. But easier doesn't offer the quality of life we deserve. After what we've experienced, after what I've seen, we have been forced into and trapped at the bottom of a deep, sunless, inescapable pit. Despair. Hell without the flames.

Tears fall, and I try not to touch my lenses as I wipe my eyes. My body shifts as stabbing pains cut through the middle of me. Immediately, I release Nikki's hand to clench my middle. I suck in a deep breath, but struggle to let it out. My air imprisoned by my pain.

I shut my eyes tightly, groan, force the breath out, easing the edge of the sharpness.

"You okay?" Nikki asks worriedly, wiping sweat from my forehead.

I nod, my focus on my breathing, on pushing through this pain brought on by emotional wounds I fear will never heal.

Nikki's hand slowly finds its way back to mine. "I got you."

No, I tell myself. *Get through this moment. Pull your shit together, Malachi. Don't put this on her.*

I lower my head. A chilly fall breeze dances across my face, hopefully drying the fresh sweat beads.

Nikki lowers her head again too. Though my hand is clammy, she doesn't pull away. "It hits me like that too," she whispers. "I see his face, see his tears, and then get stabbed through the gut, through the heart. Sometimes, it even feels like the air is being choked out of me."

I hold her hand more firmly, hoping to communicate, *I got you.* While I may not seem capable in this moment, I can provide a safe, loving place for someone who is desperately trying to look like something they're not. Whole.

I, too, am walking around disguised as someone healed and mostly together, surviving the negativity of Dolorville's duplicitous saints. No one here will understand Nikki like I do. We're one in the same, grieving losses and trying to survive being different in a place we aren't allowed to be.

"She went from the faggot to a cursed mute."

Simultaneously, our heads rise, and our four eyes pierce those of someone I used to pray alongside in Sunday school. Standing beside his Bible-toting mother, I see someone who used to eye me intently, but never spoke ill of me, at least not to my face. Though this town has always seemed obsessive, even scary because of how rehearsed people sound, I used to believe these people understood what albinism actually is. Back when I was a kid, I believed Grandma's neighbors accepted my differences and maybe even had private talks with their kids about the impoliteness of making cruel assumptions and prying with personal questions. Unfortunately, I thought too highly of these people.

Based on the treatment I receive now, I know their private conversations were derogatory, but because I didn't live here, was protected by two fearless parents, and had Drew's strong personality by my side, rumors never got back to me. I was left in the dark about how they really felt about me, which I'm unafraid to admit, was a great place to be. Right now, I wouldn't mind walking blindly again.

Nikki snatches her hand from mine. "What the fuck did you just say? Say it again, Abraham! I went from what to what?" she asks loudly, her tone threatening, forcing Abraham to stand mute, the thing he just insulted me for being.

I grab Nikki, not in as strong of a grip as I'd grab a man, but I take hold of her arm and pull her back.

"Nikolette!" Abraham's mother steps in front of her near-grown son, her pointer finger extended. "Your mother is going to hear about this. You should not be using that type of language, especially in front of your betters." She shakes her head disappointedly as though she's been harmed. "I just can't imagine the pain you must be putting your mother through. You've been so misled since Joseph took his wrong turn. Now, you're no longer attending service and surrounding yourself with other troubled people."

I wish this stutter would go away so I could tell this woman to go straight to hell.

Nikki's face twists. "You're not my better. You're my elder. Just another old fanatic in demand of respect and submission, yet you refuse to show it to other people. You may be older than us, but Joseph was still a person, deserving of respect and kindness. And Malachi..." She glances at me before turning back to Abraham's mother. "How can you let your son talk about someone who just lost their family? How can you stand silently, allowing your son to bully another, just to go smile in his grandmother's face?"

I've wanted to ask so many people in this town those exact questions.

Nikki pulls her arm from my hold. "You know what? Tell my mama. While you're talking to her,

I'm going to walk Malachi home, so I can talk to his grandmother. Ms. Ida should know how her friends are allowing their children to treat her only living grandson."

Nikki and I stand side by side before Joseph's grave. On the pathway that leads from one end of the cemetery to the other, Abraham's mother stands, covered in a formal overcoat, lined in faux fur. With her head lowered and her eyes on her Bible, she appears almost ashamed. Behind her, her coward son stands. His eyes, absent of remorse, are on his mother, his enabler.

"He's not cursed," Nikki says sternly. "He's albino. You can't catch it. He's not the result of some spell. He's not evil." She jabs her finger at them as she makes each point. "Malachi is a normal person. Maybe you'd both know that if you took the time to educate yourselves. Try a new book some time. I don't think God will strike you down for learning about something He created."

Abraham's mother's rage-filled eyes find Nikki's. Her nostrils expand. Her lips part, prepared to respond.

Nikki adds quickly, "God made what you're letting your son insult. God made what you're judging every day. If we all come from God, like your good ol' pastor preaches," she says condescendingly, "then you have to accept that the faggot and the cursed mute were two of his unique designs too."

Abraham's mother gasps. Her heels drag along the path as she walks back the way they came, barely lifting her feet with each step. Nikki's words must've robbed them of their interest in paying respects to whoever they came to visit, but I don't let that concern me. Loaded words should be treated like any other weapon. If you decide to attack someone armed with your weapon, it should be embedded in your mind that the other person could have something too. Something capable of causing even more damage.

Swiftly, Nikki turns to me. Ripples form between her brows, and suddenly regret takes up residence in her eyes, making me question her with mine.

"I didn't mean what I said. I know you're not a cursed mute."

I nod, unoffended, but instead appreciative of the blunt repetition Nikki used for emphasis.

She sighs. "I feel for you, Malachi. I know you want to scream and tell everyone how you feel, but nothing you say or don't say will ever be right in their eyes," she grumbles with a shrug. "They attack you for not speaking, but for fuck's sake, if you try to defend yourself and they hear you stutter, they'll be calling you a retard next."

I don't type. No need to tell her I agree with everything she's saying. We both know the truth about this town. I'm unordinary in a place where uniqueness is an unwritten crime. The cruelest of words are reserved for those who don't fit into

Dolorville's old-fashioned mold. Wicked words I would never be allowed to say are only acceptable when I'm on the receiving end. My feelings will never matter to these people because I'm unfairly viewed as damned as opposed to what I really am and should be welcomed as—different.

"And I've never called anyone a faggot or retard, Malachi. These are not words I'd ever say, but that bitch…"

I reach out, grab her hand, and hope the understanding I feel can be read across my face.

Her eyes appear more relaxed, but still remain puppy-like. Apologetic.

I pull out my phone and type, *Don't apologize for doing the right thing. I'm not offended. I'm grateful. Her son spit those words out. If it was okay for him to say them, she shouldn't have an issue with you shoving them down her throat.*

She shakes her head. "The right thing would've been to cuss that old bitch out. But…" She shakes her head and releases a loud, grunt-filled sigh. "My mama did teach me better than to cuss out my elders. I can't agree with all of her teachings, but that one has stuck." Nikki chuckles sarcastically. "The person that hag wants to snitch on me to is the only reason I didn't verbally annihilate her. The things I could throw in her and her son's faces." Nikki shakes her head again.

I remain quiet, offering no typed or non-verbal responses, just listening ears.

"Ignorant bastards," Nikki mumbles. "My mama is so tired of hearing about me from everyone. She was tired of me before Joseph killed himself," she admits. "But Mama must know something about what I feel is right. I know she's going easy on me because I'm still grieving, but even when Joseph was still here and the gay rumors were circulating, she didn't punish me for being his friend and outspoken ally. At some point, she's going to either ask me to leave or jump on board with my way of thinking and come to terms with the fact that this town, her people, and these ludicrous ways of thinking, are not only outdated, but outrageous."

Still, I refrain from typing, allowing her to vent.

"But," she says, letting out a deflated sigh. "Mama's likely to ask me to leave before I'm ready to leave him."

Being exiled from Dolorville sounds like a gift, but I guess I can understand the anchor of a broken heart.

I want to tell Nikki what I'm sure she already knows, that Joseph would want her as far away from here as possible, but fear and determination are holding her captive. She's terrified of leaving him the way everyone else has. She needs to see some form of justice prevail, to see sociopaths held accountable for Joseph's demise. She's waiting for what I'm waiting for. The impossible.

We slowly follow the single path out of the cemetery. We leave behind the voiceless and head for Grandma's.

Do me a favor, Nikki, I type as we stroll. *Hold off on talking to my grandmother until after my trip to the old theater. I don't know if she already knows or how she may react to learning what her people are saying about me, but I need to be able to sit at Mama's side, just in case my grandma wants to share that info with her. Trust me, my mama has been dealt all she can stand.*

Nikki reads my message quickly. "No problem at all. Whatever you need, I got you. Now and always." Her tone is filled with that special Nikki sweetness that sounds almost motherly. "I was actually just throwing that out as a threat. If you don't want me to say anything at all, I won't. You've got it hard enough, which is what baffles me about the treatment you get. Joseph too," she adds. "After going through so much, these crazies still can't show kindness and love for another human." She throws her hands up. "Scratch that. I'd even take pity for you guys. Anything would be better than being victimized over and over again."

Here she goes again, giving love and forgetting what she's deserving of too. Nikki, with an all-accepting, open heart, ironically isn't treated as she should be *because* of that loving heart. She is viewed as a disappointment here in Dolorville. She befriended a homosexual, openly defended him, and committed the ultimate sin. She abandoned the church. Now, she's seen walking around with an albino, a supposed cursed guy. She doesn't only stand at my side, she defends me, and at times, our hands find each other's and we don't let go. While all of these things may be unacceptable to her elders, she's lost her dearest friend, and her final opportunity to say goodbye was taken away when his father forbade a public funeral. Her very real and human pain is dismissed because of the company she keeps. What she feels Joseph and I deserve, she does too. However, we live in a place I'm shocked exists. This tiny, unprogressive town is one of the most isolating places on Earth where differences make you evil and acceptance makes you an outcast. This community, full of small minds, kills. What a town without pity can do.

I type, *Don't tell my grandma unless Abraham's mother talks to your mom. If not, it's whatever. I don't plan on staying here after graduating. Let 'em all talk.*

"Make it to graduation for me, please, Malachi. I know this place is man-eating. I know, for us, this is the unhappiest place on Earth, but hang in there. Not just for me, but for your mama. Once she starts to heal, and she will," Nikki says surely, "I need you to get her out of here. Even though everyone goes to church and says they're living beautiful lives, no one laughs. I noticed the other day, my mother doesn't even smile. Aren't happy people supposed to do happy shit?"

Eagerly, I type a question I researched during the late-night hours while trying to keep from seeing flashbacks of the worst day of my life. *Do you know what dolor means?*

Nikki shakes her head as she reads my question. "You mean dolor, like Dolorville? I always thought of it as just this town's name. Never put too much thought into it. Why?"

I type, *Last night, I got curious and looked it up. Google the definition.*

She takes my phone and does just that. Her eyes bulge as she learns that dolor is defined as a state of great sorrow or distress. I was surprised upon reading that as well, but felt that everything about this town makes the name befitting. Happiness can't exist in distress, which is why it can't make a home here.

Nikki and I walk, and like other times, find comfort in holding hands. Unashamed, she walks beside the guy with no pigment, with hair uncut and yellow, with brows and a thin goatee to match. Even with my protective eyewear and a stutter that has silenced me, she's here, being what I've missed having. A friend.

Dolorville is home to so much no one should be proud of, but it's also where Nikki was born. If someone like Nikki could be from here and maintain the type of heart and mind she possesses, Dolorville can't be as evil as I've grown to believe.

While I'm convinced spaces hold energy, just as people do, the darkness and gloom that haunts Dolorville wasn't and isn't strong enough to break down Nikki. Of all the things Dolorville has smashed into nothingness, Nikki is still here. No matter who she faces off against, they're forced to face themselves, their own ugliness. They're unmasked and dragged out of their preferred hiding place—Denial.

In every other way, Dolorville lives up to its dreadful name, but there isn't an absence of sunshine here. She may not have anything to smile about right now, but Nikki is seen and felt no matter who's trying to avoid her. I'm holding hands with the brightest ray Dolorville's seen since my mother's departure. Unbreakable and at my side is Dolorville's clearest mirror.

IDA GRACE

On my back, I lie silently, waiting for Grandma to peek her head in to ensure I'm asleep. She stops by Mama's room first, prays over her daughter, then walks in to check on me. She doesn't pray aloud in my room as she does Mama's, but she checks in nightly without fail.

I'm never asleep when she checks in, but I prefer to pretend that I am to avoid one-sided conversations and lengthy Bible readings. I lie still, eyes closed, and after the door shuts behind her, I practice speaking, often stuttering myself into a crying ball of frustration, missing the voice I worked so hard to develop.

Lazily, I allow my head to fall to the side. I stare at the blinking time on my alarm clock, its glow the only light in this small, wood panel-lined room. Right beside it sits my welcome gift from Grandma. I run my hand across the cover and wipe away any dust that may have settled on a Bible that hasn't been opened since I moved here.

I remember a time when I'd read The Bible on my own, a time when I'd pray in the middle of the day just to give thanks. Now, I'm more disconnected than ever from my faith. Since that

TAMMY FEREBEE

Friday, when the smell of murder filled the air, my
lungs, and ultimately my memory, I've struggled to
talk to God, to read *The Good Book,* to even
understand where I stand in terms of my faith. I
lack the strong, familiar connection to it, and I
can't seem to get past the anger I feel toward Him.
I feel cheated, robbed. I feel like I deserve answers
and understanding, and until I get them, until I
understand why they needed to be taken from us,
and why my life had to become this, I can't go back
to that faith-filled boy I once was.

The door creaks open mid-thought, giving me
a start, forcing my eyes to dart to my
grandmother's.

"Why are you still awake? Something ailing
you?" she asks, her voice sweet, carrying a deep
Southern accent Drew and I used to mimic. "You
ill?" she questions as she enters.

I shake my head.

She slowly eases down and sits on the side of
the bed, never reaching for the light chain dangling
from my lamp to brighten the space. "Your mama's
been asleep for a while. I don't even think she took
her pill."

I nod; I know she did. I put it in her mouth
and then held a glass of water to her lips to help her
get it down.

"Oh, she did take it?" she asks, sounding
almost relieved.

Again, I nod. *Always.* I hate that she needs medication to calm herself and to help her sleep through the night, but it's better than her lying in the dark, crying for hours on end. She will always take it. I'll make sure of it.

"You're a good son to her, Malachi," she says gently. "I watch how careful, how patient..." Her voice cracks and her head falls. "I see you parent my child, doing what I can't. Just looking at her is doing something to me I've never experienced."

I push myself upright, stunned at the emotion she's sharing in front of me. Even at my grandfather's funeral, Grandma didn't shed a tear and almost scolded *us* for showing emotion. She wanted us to be happy that he was now free from the ugliness of the Earth and able to dance on both legs, no longer a slave to his diabetes. This is a surprising, unfamiliar side of her, but a welcomed one. Her daughter, now unrecognizable, is suffering both physically and emotionally on a daily basis, right before her eyes. Not seeing Grandma break has angered me, has made me question the existence of her heart. But I see it now. It's been tucked behind a steel wall of prayer and strength, but vulnerability is rearing its head in this dark room.

I place my hand on my grandmother's back, trying to offer her support without making her uncomfortable by wrapping her in a tight, and possibly unwanted, hug.

"I owe you an apology, Malachi." She sniffles. The darkness hides her tears. "You've taken on more than you should, and I've been practically sleeping at the church, trying to figure out how to pray this pain away." She pulls a balled-up tissue from her robe pocket and wipes her nose. "It's not going away. It's not getting any easier to carry. It's killing me!" she hollers out, her voice cracking horribly. "My daughter is no longer alive in there! She's breathing, but her life was taken with her husband's, with Andrew's. And you," her voice becomes gentle. "You need so much I can't give you, so much she can't give you right now."

Slowly, I pull my hand from her back and clasp my hands together, trying to calm the shaking. I can't imagine what she has in mind. Whatever treatment I may require, it's not here in this town. It's not in her church.

Grandma's head falls again. "I don't know what to do. I don't want my daughter medicated forever, and I'm terrified that she's going to end up hospitalized and treated like she's out of her mind. I think she could really use some prayer, have blessed hands lain upon her, but the pastor won't…" She falls silent, shakes her head, reuses her tissue. "I just feel like if he were to come here, it'd make a world of difference."

No the hell it wouldn't. I shake my head. I can't pretend that this is even remotely okay with me. Grandma doesn't realize it, but she's leaping over a line I won't even allow her to step over. My mama will not be insulted. She will not be emotionally neglected should she decide to open up. She will not be on the receiving end of his condescending tone or have to digest his offensive remarks about a pain he can't empathize with. She will not endure what I have.

I grab my phone, click on my notepad, and in all caps, I type, *HE'S NOT GOD.*

She pulls back, eyes bulging, mouth open.

I take a deep breath, prepare to be slapped off the bed, to hear the never-ending defense of this town's fiend. I sit on edge, ready to hear how wonderful he is and how life-changing his preaching is. I wait to hear her say everything I've already heard, and I prepare to share my honest thoughts, something I've never been brave enough to do before now.

She exhales loudly. "I don't view him as God, but he is godly. He is a chosen one."

I erase the message in all caps and type, *He chose himself, Grandma. There is nothing godly about a man who wouldn't walk down the street to pray with a woman who lost most of her family. There is nothing godly about a man who believes my stutter is made up and is my way of seeking benefits. There is nothing godly about a man who would allow his own son to be ostracized and belittled because of his sexual orientation.*

She shakes her head, throws her hands up. "Joseph is not up for discussion. I can't speak on what goes on in someone else's household. I reckon people could've treated him better, but I can only speak for myself. I prayed for that young man, which is all I could do. He wasn't mine to talk about or talk to. But you," She points. "You're my blood, and you are up for discussion, one we're fin' to have right here and now."

No slap. No discipline. I try to blink the shock from my face.

"I didn't know he felt that way about your stutter, Malachi. You should've come here and told me. All he mentioned was that you weren't opening up to him at all. I didn't know he..." Her cracking voice returns. "I can understand why you wouldn't open up to someone who's accusing you of faking an impediment."

I reach out to my grandmother, and she places her beautiful brown hand atop my pale palm.

"I'm sorry, baby. I haven't done right by you."

I scooch forward to wrap my grandmother in a secure embrace. It's true, she hasn't done right by me, but I haven't by her either. I didn't tell her what my life has truly been like here. I didn't give her the chance to prove that she would choose me.

She whispers three more apologies in my ear, and I tear up. Her guilt is palpable, and I rub her back, hoping it translates as my acceptance.

"I have to share something with you, something that may change how you feel about me."

We slowly detach. Jitters run all over my body as I nervously await her words.

She inhales deeply before releasing a mouthful of air in my face. My nose twitches at the strong smell of mouthwash on her breath. "*I* made these people afraid of you," she says, her voice so faint I can barely hear it.

My face scrunches as confusion overtakes me.

"Years ago, your mother and father took a delayed honeymoon to Africa. Your mother had wanted to go for years, but we couldn't afford it. And aside from the money, I talked about it with some friends, and they told me about malaria, human trafficking, wild animal attacks, undrinkable water. I refused to even consider it after hearing about all that." She takes another deep breath, doesn't look at me as she speaks, keeps her head lowered. "But your father took her over there anyway. Andrew was a year old and stayed here with me. And..." She clears her throat. "You were conceived on that trip," she shares, something my parents had already told me. "When I first saw you, I was terrified, Malachi. Absolutely terrified of you."

My stomach sinks. I didn't know that.

"I didn't know if they were cursed while they were over there. I didn't know what had happened for you to come out like...like..." she fumbles over her words, waves her hand in a circular motion trying to think of the most appropriate term. "This." She looks at me briefly. "So different."

107

A knot fills my throat. I turn to my left, quickly scan the bedside table. No water here to drink it away, just a thick, dry pain making me want to release tears.

"I wouldn't hold you," she admits, shaking her head. "I named you like I did Andrew, but I couldn't wrap my arms around you. I couldn't kiss you. Even though your parents tried to educate me and repeatedly told me that albinism isn't contagious, isn't wrong, isn't evil, I couldn't get those thoughts out of my mind."

I want to ask where she heard these myths, how she came to associate albinism with being cursed. While I'm aware that there are countless hurtful myths that have been passed on for generations, leading to albinos being hunted, attacked, and killed, especially in Africa, little about the world and its variety of people seems to be discussed in Dolorville. Other than recited scriptures, church activities, and community gossip, nothing else seems to be brought up. I'm surprised that here of all places, albinism is even heard of, which only shows how far and wide hurtful, fear-based untruths can travel.

Mr. Wallace's comment at the pharmacy was less shocking to me. Albinos are born with an inherited condition. Michael Jackson, born brown, was diagnosed with vitiligo later in life. Two different conditions mashed together to mean the same thing by the uneducated, both often criticized by those who want to hurt others who aren't like them.

"So," she continues. "During prayer requests at the church, I told them about your condition, about where you were conceived, and asked them to stand with me in prayer. Before you were even brought here, Joseph's grandfather, our pastor at the time, had sat me down for a talk. He had told me the importance of bringing you into the church to see how you'd react."

How I'd react? Like I'm the fucking kid from the movie, The Omen?

"He also wanted to bless you in a holy place." She cocks her head. "Well, that's what he said, but I think he was afraid of you, too. We had just never seen one in real life."

I shake my head, floored by what I'm hearing.

"Your parents weren't having it. Your mama kept you out of Dolorville for a long while, worried about how you'd be received. And you know your father wasn't gonna allow his kids to be spoken about just any ol' kinda way, so I had to bond with you in your home. Even there, I was still distant." She briefly pauses and sucks in a deep breath. "But it was during that time I had become most grateful for Andrew. You see, I had already built such a strong bond with him. He was my first grandbaby!" she cries out. "I couldn't not see him, so I visited y'all fairly often and watched how you were so accepted and adored by your parents, their friends, and your big brother. Andrew would kiss you until the point of tears. He just couldn't leave you alone. You were his baby," she says, chuckling through her tears. "I watched how no one feared you. Your parents took you to church. Nothing remarkable happened."

Really? You mean, there was no need for an exorcism? Go figure.

"So, I realized something I had convinced myself of just wasn't true. Finally, I took you in my arms." She holds her tissue to her nose. "I remember holding you for the first time and hearing you cry because you didn't know me. It broke me. I wanted to cry too, but your brother was there, watching my every move with you struggling in my arms. Andrew was only a toddler and climbed right up in my lap and said, *'You okay, you okay'* in the sweetest voice."

Tears fall from my eyes in the dark as well.

"He calmed you down, and you let me hold you as long as you could see him. And from then on, just like my sweet Andrew, I just couldn't let you go. You were my grandbaby too. Just special enough to make the world take a second look."

I wipe my tears away, but more replace them just as quickly. I don't have many memories without Andrew. He was literally my day one, my first friend, my best friend, my protector. I've lost someone I thought I'd ultimately leave this world with. Now, he's on the other side without me, and I couldn't feel lonelier. I've always loved my brother, but I didn't realize how big of a part he played in my life until he was no longer in it. A piece of me is gone, and no matter who enters my world, they won't be able to fill that emptiness.

"I say all that to say, I'm sorry, baby. Malachi, you didn't deserve a cold welcome to the world from your own grandmother, and I'm fixin' to make sure you're treated the way you deserve to be while you're here. I will be having a word with the pastor and searching for another counselor for you. Believe me, I didn't know everything he was saying to you, but he did tell me you walked out on him. He didn't offer me any details, not even what may have triggered you. He kept speaking of confidentiality, but he's overshared about your past visits, detailing the scriptures he recited to you and the topics he focused on. Suddenly, not sharing felt pretty odd." She slides her hand over and squeezes mine. "I want to do right by you. I love you."

I love you too, Grandma. Through all of your misguidance and hurtful mistakes, even those undeserved slaps, I've loved you.

I don't type the words, just sit very still, allowing the tears to fall. I'll tell her, but right this second, I want to fully absorb and process this apology. *I'm sorry* and *I love you* remain two of the hardest things for many to say. She just said them both, and in doing so, has made me feel like I don't only have Nikki here, but her too.

"I want to heal, Malachi. I want to breathe without this pain weighing on me so heavy. I want to hear my daughter's voice again, even if I have to hear her cussin' folks out."

With my free hand, I cup my face under my eyes and sweep my tears away in one slow wipe until many are absorbed into my short goatee.

"And I think I know what to do," she says, squeezing my hand, trembling as she sobs. "I need to take y'all back home, and we need to fight. We need to fight like hell."

My eyes widen, and a high-pitched squeal unexpectedly escapes me. *Hell.* I'm taken aback by the word choice. My reverent grandmother still disciplines my mother for swearing. This is the first time I've ever heard her say anything even slightly profane.

"The world needs to see your face, see your race, see our grief, hear our anger. I'll speak for the family. If you're okay with that," she adds, seeking my permission, but not waiting for it. "I'll tell them about your stutter, about your mama's breakdown. I'll tell them what that animal did to us, what he took from us. I know, without a shadow of a doubt, that the protesters and supporters will stand behind us again. Things may have quieted down in the media, but that's because we are the fire needed to keep things going, the voices needed to make things happen. They're waiting on us, Malachi. It may be true that we have a lot of work to do amongst ourselves within the Black community, but what people can't deny is our ability to come together to fight for justice and the rights of our brothers and sisters. The Black community is a force, and I want us to use our power to cage that racist. I want my grandson's face to circulate again, but this time *we'll* control the narrative. No more talk about marijuana. I want the world to hear about his grades, his friendships, how he cut the grass for his elders without pay, his basketball skills, and his brotherhood with you. I want your father to be known as a provider, a loving parent, a dedicated husband who I wholeheartedly trusted to take care of my daughter for the entirety of her life. And you, Malachi, I want to kill the narrative that your skin saved your life. Your mama told me weeks before that Friday how that racist pig often provoked you as well. You're still here because you were home. Your pigment didn't save your life. Your location did."

As I listen to Grandma, I envision the protestors standing behind us as she speaks on behalf of our family. I see myself at her side, listening closely as her thick accent and local word choices reveal where she was brought up. I imagine seeing our names trending and her words shared across social media. I visualize my mother's strength resurfacing as she sees and hears us fighting. The very thought of Mama making her first formal public statement and using her voice again makes me shudder. I know that woman. If I'm out there, no matter how slowly she may move, she's going to find the ability to stand on the front line with me, to fight for our family, hand in hand.

"Are you ready?" Grandma asks. Her question distracts me from my thoughts and makes me fully rejoin her back in this room.

I nod. I'm beyond ready. As a matter of fact, we're late, but we're still coming. My mother had to have gotten her strength from somewhere, and I'm ready to see the version of my grandmother I've never been introduced to before.

"Your school presentation is tomorrow evening, right?"

I nod. Our short film is complete, edited, and ready to be shown.

"And Nikolette has offered to drive you and bring you back. Is that right?"

Again, I nod. Nikki has been given permission to borrow her mother's car and is gung-ho to drive me there, wait in the car, and bring me back. I think her eagerness is to get out of Dolorville, but not alone, with someone who can empathize with her, with someone else who knew Joseph and didn't see him as a walking sin.

"Nikolette has her own struggles going on. If something changes, or she doesn't feel up to the drive, I'll take you over yonder and come back for you." She points toward the small window as though the theater is within our line of vision. "Regardless, you'll get there. And on Monday, I'll call the school and have them excuse your absence, because we need to get the ball rolling. We'll start calling news stations, maybe you could update your old social media pages, and we can schedule some interviews."

I reach in once again to wrap my grandmother in a hug. This time, she rubs my back, and in this moment, I feel a foreign closeness to her. The love I've always had for her didn't necessarily make me feel bonded with her, but on this night, in this dark, barely lit room, I no longer feel separated by distance or decades. I'm sitting with my family, my ally. I'm meeting my grandmother for the first time, and I couldn't be more pleased to make the acquaintance of Ms. Ida Grace.

WHITE

The ride is mostly silent; the only noise filling the car is the low playing music whispering through the speakers and the random clicking of the broken cassette player. Nikki has barely spoken, but the space doesn't feel awkward, doesn't feel tense. It's a comfortable quiet I haven't experienced in a while, especially next to someone I want at my side.

My quiet moments typically scream at me. In the dark, in a space that'd sound silent to other listening ears, my shortcomings relentlessly taunt me to the point of tears, making my efforts at improving upon them feel pitiful. The endless gunshots sound off inside my mind, and the small space of my room smells of warm blood, of death, of trauma, of rage. Lying next to an untouched Bible in the small room, lined in wood paneling, I always find myself back on my old street, kneeling beside my family, covered in their blood, surrounded by the faces and voices of those who love me. Quiet, for me, is anything but after that Friday.

Nikki taps against the steering wheel as we sit at a red light. I watch her pointer finger tap slowly and repetitively as her other fingers remain wrapped around the side of the wheel. As her fingers drum a soft beat, my fingertips tingle. I want to hold her hand, to keep it in mine, to feel even closer to her. Though this car is carrying broken spirits, Nikki makes my brokenness feel more bearable. Though my pieces are shattered, some not even here, somehow, I feel slightly together when I'm with her. I feel heard without having to speak, comforted without being touched, understood without having to explain.

My eyes fall from her fingers and return to my phone screen where I continue to note-take, incapable of getting last night's conversation with Grandma out of my head. I bullet the key points I want her to discuss when we begin calling for the attention of the public. Exhuming my family's story has to be done right. We need the world to hear our truth, what's happening behind our closed doors, to understand the gravity of our newfound reality, to be reminded that bullets tear apart a lot more than flesh.

I type what I want her to say. *Skin color is not race. Two Black parents cannot birth a white child. Albinism is why my grandson, Malachi, lacks pigment. It's why his hair is yellow, why his skin requires protection from the sun, why his eyes are sensitive to bright lights, why his skin is fairer than most white people. It's not an ethnicity. It's not a race. It's an inherited disorder and in no way contributed to my grandson's survival. On that Friday afternoon, on the day that ruined my family and shattered us in ways we didn't think possible, Malachi and my daughter were in their home. They weren't "spared" by Bennett Dickson. They simply weren't present. My son-in-law, eldest grandson, and their dog were innocent victims. Their lives were taken from them. Not because they were harassing the Dicksons. Not because they were making the community uncomfortable for their neighbors to live in. They were ripped from this world and prevented from reaching their full potential because they were born Black in a world that doesn't love color.*

My eyes repeatedly move across the first line of my quickly typed words, *Skin color is not race.* While I expect my grandmother to receive some backlash for that controversial line, I do hope it encourages people to think before judging those they pass. Albinos have white skin, but many of us aren't white. There are Native Americans who have such a deep, dark chocolate tone, they're perceived as Black. In my old school, a Dominican teammate of mine was darker than my Nigerian friends, leading many to disrespectfully question the story of where he was born.

Each of our complexions tells a unique story, but it's often one that requires more than a glance to understand. While I wish people could stop judging altogether, I realize the impossibility of that, so as a start, it'd be nice if people's judgments were at least based on facts.

"You excited about your film debut?" Nikki asks as we approach.

I nod, my eyes focused on what's before us.

We slowly approach the theater tucked in between two small shops. One is named The Fish Bowl, the other, The Creamery. Both stores glow from within, but the theater doesn't. The outdoor ticket booth is dark and unoccupied. The marquee isn't lit and looks as if it's been left untouched. The black lettering is hard to make out at first glance, but as we move closer, can be read. In bold black letters, *Final Show* is spelled out.

I almost question if we're in the right place, as the theater still looks abandoned, but I spot a school bus further up the street, then recognize familiar faces, classmates I despise, exiting their vehicles.

Nikki pulls up behind a silver Toyota Camry, its flashers on as one of my schoolmates steps out of the passenger seat. My eyes move from the back of the modern hybrid parked in front of us and slowly begin scanning the interior of the car I'm sitting in. The luxuries I've grown used to seeing in vehicles don't exist in this one. Though my grandmother lives almost as modestly as her neighbors, she did trade in her old Saturn for something with a few extra comforts. In here, there are no touchscreens, no cameras to assist with parking, not even a CD player. The malfunctioning cassette player, still holding on to some of the ribbon from a Kirk Franklin tape, clicks randomly. The car windows must be manually rolled up and down using a crank, and according to Nikki, they stick on the way back up, forcing passengers into arm workouts.

I'm not concerned with what my classmates will think of me pulling up in what they'll likely consider a busted hooptie, but I do often wonder why Grandma, Nikki's mother, and Dolorville's other residents do the bare minimum for themselves. Their tithes have certainly taken care of the pastor. Now that Grandma seems a bit more open, perhaps I'll ask her a question I've been keeping to myself for quite some time; *Are you required to suffer in order to be considered a good Christian, and if so, why is the pastor flourishing more than anyone else in his congregation?*

"I'm so excited for you," Nikki says unenthusiastically, pulling me from my thoughts. "I'm not sure what the response will be, but you've created something that should generate an emotional response in any normal human being. It's undeniable, something to be proud of."

Though I've always looked forward to my film debut, I never thought it'd take place this way, in front of peers who fear me, gossip about me, and isolate me daily. I never thought it'd be in front of a teacher who most likely won't appreciate the message. Not because it isn't significant, but because he gets something out of challenging me.

I share Nikki's sentiment. I'm excited to slap every viewer in the face with some hard truths, but I'm equally as unenthusiastic. The feelings I want my audience to be left with, they may not feel simply because of who's delivering the message. It's not farfetched that they may not even care. It seems easy for many to turn away from things that don't affect them personally. Though I'm trying not to manifest eye rolling, sighs, and napping viewers, I'm preparing for what could realistically happen. No matter what, though, I know Melody and I have created something timeless. When it comes to the quality and depth of our short film, my confidence is unshakeable. Doubt hasn't knocked on my door, and it won't be making any visits tonight. What we're sharing is the truth of silenced voices, of restless souls.

"Loving the Malcolm X shirt too," Nikki compliments, her eyes on one of my most treasured gifts.

Receiving the shirt couldn't have come at a more perfect time. I had just finished reading *The Autobiography of Malcolm X* and was left briefly satisfied with the new information I had learned. That is, until I was struck with an unbelievable curiosity to learn even more about the misunderstood leader. My new and unquenchable thirst to learn everything I could about Brother Malcolm urged me to re-watch the film, *Malcolm X,* several times, to research him more than ever before, to binge documentaries in my free time, and to share everything I discovered with my family, almost obsessively. My information dumps, some repetitive, encouraged family discussions about our history that made me ignore even Denise's calls.

It was on my birthday, not too long after my Malcolm X obsession began, that Drew held a gift bag in front of me. I knew it must've been something he was proud to give me, as he demanded that I open it last. Usually, my parents pushed him to go first, as their birthday gifts were always the *wow* of our special days, the grand finales, the surprises we didn't expect but definitely wanted. On this particular birthday, Drew couldn't be persuaded. After receiving a new laptop from my parents, I opened Drew's present and immediately gasped, bringing the widest smile to his face. Up until then, a plain, long-sleeved tee and jeans, or a hoodie and sweats, had always been my go-to outfits, but the sight of my new gift changed that instantly.

More than any of my other shirts, I wear this one most often. Newspaper print covers every inch of it, sharing information about the slain leader. Atop the print is a large, centered image of Brother Malcolm, his finger extended and his lips parted as if he's been frozen in time, mid-speech.

I let out a long sigh, remembering Drew's smile, knowing I'll never see it again in real-time. It's not fair that he isn't here, and as proud as I am of my project, it shouldn't be presented in this theater. I should be pulling up to the high school I walked into as a nervous fourteen-year-old. I should be presenting in front of my long-time friends and shaking my head at Mama's over-the-top, loud, and proud cheers.

Nikki grabs my hand. "Thinking about your family?"

I nod. *Always.*

"They're watching, Malachi. Drew and your pop are always with you, and they wouldn't miss your premiere."

Are they? I never feel them. I'm not sure where I stand in terms of my faith, but I have tried to hold onto the belief that my deceased loved ones are in a better place, watching over me. Privately, I've asked for signs, begged my brother and father to prove they can hear my thoughts, whispers, cries. But nothing. No flickering lights. No random smells. No whispers in the dark. They don't feel present. They feel like yesterday's rain. Gone so quickly and easily forgotten by most, except by those who depend on the drops to feel something.

I hold onto Nikki's hand, thinking about someone else who seems easily forgotten by the world but doesn't deserve to be. *Joseph.* I don't want Drew, Pop, and Rocko to be the only three names trending next week. I want Nikki to come with us, to fight alongside us, to release her tears and anger for the world to see, to reveal the hell that exists in unholy Dolorville.

Deservingly so, I want Joseph's name to be on the lips of millions, his story to be retold, but honestly. And just as importantly, if not more, I want Joseph's father, the masked pastor, to feel the heat of everyone's silent accusations. I want the world to understand there's more work to be done, even in the tiny towns many don't realize still exist.

Still exist. I shake my head, exasperated, just thinking about the homophobia and racism still killing innocents around the globe. I exhale, feeling not relief, but incredulity, that in this technology-driven age, with a wealth of knowledge accessible by phone, someone like me, an albino, is still so misunderstood. I'm not the first. Not the last. We albinos are all over the world, yet we're rarely discussed and completely excluded from most educations. Deserving of acceptance, all too often, we're unfairly faced with discrimination and willful ignorance.

Well, do something about it, I say to myself. *What would Pop do?* I don't have to think long. He'd speak up. He'd educate. He'd fight to make a difference, to bring attention to what requires change. That's who I came from. That strength and bravery is in me. *Time to stand up.*

People may laugh, may walk away impatiently, but I was raised to use the most powerful thing I own. My voice. I was raised to speak up, stutter and all.

For seven months, I've been buried inside myself, cemented in grief. During the evenings, after practicing my speech behind closed doors, I ultimately go to sleep feeling like a failure, but that's not a good enough excuse to stand quietly

125

behind Grandma, especially if I'm going to ask Nikki to fight for Joseph. This is my time to lead, and the way my father and brother have always fought for me, I plan to fight for justice for them. Relentlessly.

I swallow before drawing in a deep breath and releasing it slowly. I look Nikki in the eye, her hand still in mine. I look at a fighter I've let speak for me enough. I have a voice, and I want to use it to ask her to stand beside me as I bring our lost loves back to life. Without a fight, we're simply letting them fade away.

I take another quiet, deep breath.

"What is it?" she asks. "Nerves?"

I swallow, massage my lower jaw. "I-I-I…" My mouth trembles, body temperature rises as doubt attempts to rear its ugly head, but I swallow a second time and prepare to begin again. I will speak, hear myself, and be heard. "I-I…" My head falls in frustration.

"It's okay," she compassionately whispers.

That's it, Nikki. Whisper. That was something I was taught in my younger years by my speech pathologist. Stutterers can often sing and whisper without their impediment interfering. I've been so focused on projecting my voice the way I used to, I forgot that whispers can still be heard. The power is in my words, not in how loudly I say them.

"Type it," she says.

"No," I say quietly, lifting my head, making eye contact again.

The corners of Nikki's mouth rise into an encouraging, closed-lipped smile. "Well, then, let's hear it."

A tear falls from my eye as I feel a small smile awaken on my face. At this point, it's foreign to feel my mouth move this way, but I immediately recognize the feeling, the feeling of something I didn't expect to do tonight or anytime soon.

Nikki bites her bottom lip as a tear of her own slides down her beautiful, brown face.

I whisper, "I don't want my grandma to fight for me."

Nikki leans in as she listens and nods in response to my words.

"I have to be the one. I want to be the one," I say surely, though almost inaudibly. "And I want you there."

"I will definitely be there to support you."

"No." I shake my head. "I want you there to fight for Joseph. Our people deserve more, but he needs you the way mine need me."

She doesn't respond, keeps her brown eyes on mine, and grips my hand more firmly.

"Whatever you can't say, I'll say for you. When your tears fall, I'll catch them. Whatever you need, I got you. But I need you there, Nikki. I can't do it without you."

Her hand trembles, still clutching mine.

"Nik, I didn't realize this is what I needed, or maybe I did, and I just wasn't sure that I could fight a system built against me, especially with my stutter making a surprise comeback." I shrug. "Or maybe I even thought it was pointless to fight for something rarely given to *us*. Justice. But already, I feel better, like my purpose is greater than just making it to tomorrow, taking care of Mama, and making movies. Maybe I could actually make a difference, you know? My family's deaths could possibly strengthen hate crime laws or something, and Joseph's suicide could open so many eyes. Think about it, Nik. Towns like Dolorville only get away with torturing innocent souls because nobody talks about them. People just go on like these small towns don't exist while cities are protesting and pushing for equality. It's no different than the world screaming about how horrible child molestation is, yet overlooking those polygamous compounds, separated from the rest of the world and led by Bible-waving lunatics who force children to marry grown men. If things aren't talked about, they're as good as nonexistent."

Nikki's hand continues to shake as she nods slowly, her eyes cast down. I know where the discomfort is coming from. This is no small ask. Nikki loves Joseph and has been fighting for him within Dolorville for years. Though it's created a wedge between her and her mother, it wouldn't compare to the divide it'd create if she publicly spoke against Dolorville on social media or the news. She wouldn't just be a voice for Joseph, she'd be publicly attacking her mother who's just like Dolorville's other residents—fanatical and intolerant.

I squeeze Nikki's hand, pressure being the last thing I want to put on her. My family is going to back me up as I speak out, but hers will feel ambushed and betrayed.

"Ju-Ju…" My mouth quivers, still fighting to get out the next syllable. "Ju-Ju…" I pause, take a deep breath, and remember volume control. Returning to the whisper I accidentally abandoned, I say, "Just remember, no matter what you decide, I support your decision. I feel like now is my time to get out there and be a voice for my family, but it may not be the right moment for you. When your moment comes, I'm here, whether that's tomorrow or next year."

Nikki's eyes, so full of vulnerability, find mine. "Thank you."

Gently, I take her chin in between my thumb and forefinger and softly kiss her cheek, inhaling the faint smell of baby lotion as I slowly pull back. "I gotta get in there," I tell her, my voice even lower than it was before. "Can't wait to tell you about it."

"I'll be right here. Can't wait to hear about the surprising standing ovation."

I reveal another small smile, not a forced one, an honest one, meaning more than it could ever show. Grandma's talk breathed life back into the young man my father raised, a young man Bennett's bullets weakened, but didn't kill. I'm coming back, minute by minute, and though I wish fights like this weren't necessary, I'm manifesting a victory for my family.

I release Nikki's hand before grabbing my hefty backpack from the floor, my comfort, which I plan to hold onto throughout the night.

"You can leave your backpack if you want. Don't carry what you don't need. Just take your USB."

Right away, I shake my head, my backpack still in my grasp. "I need it," I whisper.

With my bag in hand, I step out of the car, no longer in Dolorville, but back in the real world where racism exists and protection is needed. Before closing the door, I bend, look over Nikki's beautiful face, at a crush that has now come back stronger than ever. I look at who I desperately want to say something to, but don't know what. I definitely don't want to whisper *goodbye* or *see you later*. I want to say something that will let her know how I feel without being too forward or desperate-sounding.

"Okay," she says in a low voice, as though she's answering something.

Okay? I question with my face.

130

"Let's do this. Let's make some noise. Let's take these fuckers down."

I stand, briefly paralyzed at the thought of standing alongside Nikki, outside of Dolorville, at the head of protests, in the name of our loved ones.

I nod. "Together."

"I can't do it without you."

"You'll never have to," I say in a quiet voice before closing the door and sealing the heat inside with her.

Quickly, I head toward the dark theater, away from a friend I look forward to seeing in a couple of hours. Funny enough, I hadn't thought about seeing Nikki once we moved in with Grandma. I think I maybe even forgot about her, as my mind was occupied with too many other things. Now, Nikki is the most solid thing to enter my life since that Friday. We're bound by an unbreakable friendship, forged in pain.

Behind a student I recognize from class, I hastily enter the theater, trying to escape the nippy weather. Inside, the lights are dim, unseen through the tinted doors and darkened windows, and the atmosphere is missing something I mindlessly expected—the smell of popcorn to smack me in the face.

In the device that once popped the buttery movie treat lies nothing but dust and an old aluminum scoop. The glass display cases aren't lit and don't hold any sweets. As I step further in, I search for but find nothing inviting about this old space. It's simply an empty location, with a faint moist, moldy smell, filled with the ghosts of what was.

We're presenting our projects in a place that was home to many laughs, tears, first handholds, and first kisses. All touching thoughts, but I expected something different. I expected to present in an older, but still recognizable theater. This place looks more than untouched. It looks haunted.

As I scan the space from side to side, then up and down, I spot Melody standing near a set of double doors, likely the entrance to the room we'll be presenting in. With her head lowered and her focus on her phone screen, I take steps in her direction, ignoring my cell alerts, and passing by my other classmates, all standing in pairs, discussing their projects.

Melody looks up before I can tap her and loudly exhales. "I thought you weren't going to make it. I just texted you."

I reach for my phone, swipe to unlock it, and pull up my notepad, my backpack held securely in my other arm.

"No, don't read the text. I can just tell you," she says.

I wasn't checking her message, but still re-lock my phone. Like anyone else, I'm a creature of habit, but what I've started, I plan to finish. I'll be whispering my way through this evening, and before I know it, I'll be speaking at a conversational volume.

I lean in so I can be heard amongst all the chattering surrounding us, "Tell me what?" I ask.

Melody's eyes widen, almost scarily. A smile slowly stretches across her face. "Malachi, when did your speech improve? Yesterday?"

I shake my head before leaning in closer to her ear again. "The stutter is still here and thriving, but whispering is one of those speech tricks I learned years ago and forgot about. The first of many baby steps."

Her naturally downturned eyes slightly lift with happiness for my progress. "I'm so proud of you."

"I appreciate that," I whisper, with a single nod of the head. "So, what's up? Everything okay?"

Apprehension flashes across her face, stealing her smile and lowering her head.

"Hey, don't worry. Don't let your nerves get to you. I know you and I have had a few hiccups along the way, but we did this together, and it's even better than I envisioned. Almost every idea you threw out there, we used. While I focused on the message, you were thinking about all of the presentation details that are going to push our short film over the top. *We*," I repeat. "*We* did this together."

She nods, but I feel as though my authentic words have fallen on deaf ears. She doesn't look even slightly more confident. More distraught actually, now that her eyes won't look from the floor.

"And I have my USB in case he has any problems, so we don't have to worry about anything if there are any technical glitches," I say, trying again to comfort her. "He's just streaming from the school portal we uploaded the file on and then projecting the shorts onto the screen, right?"

Another silent nod from her. Feels almost like Melody and I have switched places. I'm usually the one no one can get a word out of.

"Melody, you're worrying me," I whisper, her demeanor now affecting mine.

She exhales, makes eye contact. "I know how passionate you are about this project."

Oh no. What the hell did you do?

"I know you think we submitted our final draft a few days ago, but last night, I had a stroke of genius and added a silent clip after you said you were going to bed."

I wasn't asleep all day today, so why am I just hearing about this now?

She continues, "The audio won't play, so the film is still a silent one, but I wanted something more powerful than a photo to demonstrate how the police tend to show disrespect to the families of victims in racial shootings. I feel like a clip, versus a still, best shows the harshness and ugliness of the brutality that goes beyond the victim and extends to the family as well."

Why the hell would you be nervous about sharing that with me? That sounds befitting. Something is not being said here, I think surely, leaning in to ask what.

Before I can speak, Melody says, "I hope I haven't stepped on your toes. You've made it very clear that you need to see the completed film before submission, but I think what I've added is necessary. It just wouldn't leave me alone, and I couldn't wait to ask you this morning because Mr. Roberts wasn't accepting changes after midnight, last night." Her eyes find the floor again. "A part of me feels like you're going to hate what I did, but I also kind of feel like you're going to appreciate it. Really, it's a struggle to predict how you're going to react."

"Look, Melody, if you're not pushing the bullshit narrative that I was spared or showing my deceased family, then..."

"I'm not showing your deceased family or pushing that disrespectful narrative. I promise," she interrupts me to say.

"Then why do I feel like there's more to this than what you're..."

Two loud claps grab our attention, end my whisper, and force me to swing around briskly, clutching my backpack more firmly. "Listen up, everyone!" Mr. Roberts shouts. "I'm glad everyone made it here in one piece and on time. I'm sure from the look of this place, many of you are wondering why I brought you guys to this dump?"

"Umm yeah," one of my classmates throws out, and a few others laugh.

"Well, it's actually not a dump, Lacy. This is history. All of the updated seating, food selections, various screens, and sound systems are modern day luxuries. They didn't exist back in the day, but at one point, this location offered a quality viewing experience. When you're in the theater, pay attention to the seating. Take a look at the size of the screen. I encourage you to take a guess as to how many people could be seated per viewing. Don't just create films and enjoy all the tools of the day. Remember to appreciate how films were shot in the past, how they were viewed, and what that experience was like for the public."

Many of us nod as he speaks. I'm not necessarily a fan of his, but I appreciate his thinking. Melody has my stomach twisting wildly, though.

"I know this place may not be what you had in mind, but the screen is intact and only a few of the theater seats are broken. My wife and I even rolled up our sleeves and did a little dusting in there. I think you guys will appreciate the experience."

"What about bathrooms?" John, one of my louder, nonsense-talking classmates asks.

"We won't be spending too long here. Your film projects are pretty short, but to answer your question, there are no working bathrooms inside this theater. As I stated on the permission slip, it was encouraged that you use the bathroom prior to arriving. For emergencies, which you seem to have every class period, John, I have spoken to the owner of The Creamery next door, and they were kind enough to let us use their facilities if absolutely necessary."

John laughs and turns back to his project partner, Donovan. Both are always taking lengthy bathroom breaks, goofing in the hallways, roasting people not cool enough for them, and interrupting class with corny comments.

"Any other questions before we head in?" Mr. Roberts asks.

Melody raises her hand. "What order are we presenting in?"

"I'll be drawing names randomly once everyone is seated. Anyone else?" Mr. Roberts looks around at each of us, and no one responds. "Cool," he says. "Since John brought it up, does anyone need the bathroom?"

"Not yet," John says, followed by another laugh before others chuckle too.

Fucking bunch of idiots. The cool football player laughs at his own unfunny statement, and everyone else feels like they must laugh too.

"Well, when the need arises, I have hired two security guards. One to stay on the premises and the other to escort any student next door. We're off school grounds, and it is imperative that I know where each of you are at all times. This is not a free-for-all with a bunch of running back and forth next door!" Mr. Roberts states loudly. "I decided against having parent chaperones because we'll have a viewing at school, but that doesn't mean y'all have been left in irresponsible hands. The school and your parents are very comfortable knowing future officers will be my extra eyes this evening."

No more laughter out of John.

"This is my brother, Daniel," Mr. Roberts introduces, drawing our attention to a youthful man who blended in with my classmates. "He's one of the security officers you'll see around. As the shirt states, he is currently in the Police Academy. You guys can call him Mr. Daniel if you need anything or Officer Roberts if you want to make his day."

Mr. Roberts's brother greets us with a simple wave. No words. His buzz cut, piercing blue eyes, and height all match his brother's. The clearest difference between the two is age and weight. Looking all of 21, Mr. Daniel stands beside his older brother, who is undeniably in his thirties, with more weight filling his middle. Mr. Daniel, training to protect and serve, looks like a slim college boy.

"A friend of his from the Police Academy has partnered up with him to keep an eye on things. He's..."

"Buying a few bottles of water from next door," Mr. Daniel interrupts to share.

"Well, we're not going to wait around. He should be easy to spot. He's in khakis and a dark blue button down that says Police Academy. Do not leave the premises without letting one of the three of us know."

We all nod in agreement before Mr. Roberts scoots past Melody and me to open one of the double doors. With a side head motion, he gives us the okay to enter. With Melody at my side, we walk in.

As classmates rush past me, all eager to grab the seats in the very back, I pause, my backpack squeezed tightly in my arms. Standing and taking it all in, I look around the space; the only modern things in it are Mr. Roberts's projector and laptop.

My eyes move across the rows of red, cushioned auditorium style seats, dated and worn. The last time I sat in a theater, it was beside Denise while on a double date with my brother and his girl. We sat in large, comfortable recliners, operated by buttons before a screen that took up almost an entire wall. This one is significantly smaller and white. Large, red curtains are draped on either side, and the screen is elevated and tucked back into what looks like a stage. Without a doubt, I've never seen a setup quite like this.

"Where do you want to sit?" Melody asks.

I shrug.

"Near the middle is always best, but maybe we should sit closer so we can better see. I don't know how good the quality is going to be."

I shrug again and follow Melody, her selected seating in the third row, three seats away from the aisle.

I sit, my backpack on my legs, hugged in between my arms. I remain quiet, still unsettled about Melody's surprise addition, but I refrain from offering further comfort or asking anything else about what I'm going to see shortly. I've been very headstrong about this project, and I'm sure that hasn't made me the easiest partner to work with, so tonight, I'll try to be a better team player. The last thing I want to do is badger her throughout the evening about a small clip that may take our project up a notch. I know what it feels like to be annoyed, desperately wanting to be left alone. I'm not going to be what I hate. I refuse to be her fly in the room.

Mr. Roberts moves over to his laptop to pull up an already filled-in picker wheel. "You remember where the light control is?" he asks his brother, looking toward the door.

My eyes follow Mr. Roberts's and meet those of Mr. Daniel. Leering at me from the door, Mr. Daniel stands silently, studying my face like he's uncovering an unpleasant mystery.

I briefly look away, then make eye contact again. Still with his eyes on me, he answers my teacher, "Yes, up there." He gestures with a nod.

"Cut them off for me, please."

Mr. Daniel heads up the aisle, his eyes leaving me as he passes.

"You okay?" Melody asks.

"I'm used to it," I whisper, overly familiar with that invasive stare now that I've spent so much time in Dolorville and at my new high school. Faces full of puzzlement with a hint of disgust are something I expect now.

The space darkens and my eyes remain glued to the picker wheel projected on the big screen at the front of the room. Without warning, Mr. Roberts clicks the mouse once, and the wheel spins, our names moving so quickly, they blur.

"I really don't want to go first," Melody says.

I don't reply. I wouldn't mind going first or even last. Our project will likely be the heaviest of the night. Starting with something so dark and then lightening the mood of the room with less serious films would be nice, but so would starting lighter and ending the evening with a bang. Unlike my partner, I'm okay with either.

"John and Donovan, you're up," Mr. Roberts announces.

The applause is loud, but not enough to drown out Melody's *whew* of relief. A quick peek at her, and I can't help but feel a little guilty. I don't think we'll ever be best friends, but I can't deny that she's been a dedicated partner, even after hitting a few hurdles. Never was it my intention to be so obsessive with this project and its message that I put her on edge about one small, and seemingly relevant, change.

John and Donovan's film starts. The title, *American Football.* As their short begins, starring the two of them, cheers fill the space. Random clips from within the football huddle play, followed by interviews with their coaches, then close ups of John performing victory dances in the end zone. Though verbal reactions to what's on screen are sounding off behind me, I can't find a significant point to this self-absorbed compilation.

Uninterested in their narcissistic project, my eyes begin to drift elsewhere. Near the door we entered through, Mr. Daniel leans against the wall. Quietly, he speaks to his security partner for the evening, another slim guy, cut almost bald, with his back to us. My attention leaves their private conversation and returns to the stage where the screen is housed. I look at the curtains inquisitively. *Were live plays performed in old movie theaters?* I'll have to look that up.

The roaring applause pulls me away from my random thoughts, and I clutch my bag even tighter, waiting for the noise to calm down. I don't join in. No need to applaud someone who has grimaced at me and verbally assaulted me under his breath.

John is more than the class clown. He's a bully, and because he's so popular, his behavior encourages that of his minions.

"We'll ask and answer questions at the end. Let's move on to the next film," Mr. Roberts says, clicking once to send the wheel on another whirl.

Around and around, the names blur, until the wheel slows and the arrow points to our names.

"Malachi and Melody, you're up."

We don't receive the acclamation John and Donovan did before their presentation began, but truthfully, I don't need it. Being the center of attention has never been my thing, which is why I wanted to be excluded from the film. Behind the scenes is where my best work is done.

The room falls silent, and the grandfather clock appears. Though I've seen this sequence several times by now, wildly flying butterflies fill my middle.

Seamlessly, black and white clips and still photos flow across the screen, pulling us through an ordered history of slavery, of racial violence, of LGBTQ+ hate crimes, of deadly epidemics, of natural catastrophes. Captivated by our creation, I realize I'm holding my breath, every muscle in my body tensed. In my mind, I can hear the wails of the crying mothers, the powerful pressure of fire hoses crashing into African Americans, the panic in the voices of those who feared deadly viruses. I can hear it all, can feel every emotion right alongside those who struggled before me.

As our short film moves the audience through time, the black and white slowly comes to life in color. A large Confederate flag being waved at a Klan meeting is where we decided to transition, to show that what was, still is.

While history continues to play out before me and my schoolmates, I glance at Mr. Roberts, his eyes fixated on the screen. I quickly look over at his brother and security partner. Both have their backs facing us and are watching our mini production. I don't turn in my seat, but briefly close my eyes and listen to the silence. Though my classmates are quieter than they've ever been, I don't hear boredom. I hear focus. Maybe even care.

Proud of what we've developed, I reopen my eyes and smile. Giggles and chatter aren't background noise. We did it. We've captured their attention.

This is all I wanted. Needed rather. More than an A plus, more than a standing ovation, I needed to get in their minds, their hearts, and show the parallels between one hundred years ago and now. Time hasn't stood still, but in many ways, people have. With our chosen visuals, I can only hope our film inspires introspection and a desire to be a part of forward movement. The sheer possibility that we could encourage that with a school project is beyond satisfying.

Feeling so content, so successful, I await Melody's final edit, watching images and clips we selected together, until I become like every other viewer in the room, stunned by what I'm seeing.

No quicker than it appeared, my smile fades. Looking at the addition Melody added last minute, I jerk in my seat, my back sliced open with betrayal.

I lean forward, mouth fallen open, and through stretched open eyes, peer at the photo of Mr. Thompson's house, his front door covered with the large Confederate flag I passed daily. I stare at a crime scene I was present at, my father's and brother's bodies out of view.

Palms moist, I rub where their warm blood once was. I grab my chest, recalling the excruciating pain I felt seeing my family gunned down there. I hold my breath, purposely this time, trying to escape the smell of blood and open wounds.

The photo slowly slides out of view, promptly replaced by a silent clip of me moving in between Mama and the rude cop who yelled at us at the scene. I jump to my feet, head shaking in protest. This clip isn't pushing the narrative I hate most, but I didn't want to be a part of the presentation. I was adamant about that.

My heartbeat gallops, body convulses, hands tremble, still holding on to my backpack as rage overheats me.

I put one hand out. I want to holler to stop the film, but my stutter silences me once again. I look down at Melody, fully understanding the sudden onset of her extreme discomfort. *Lying bitch.* She took control of a situation, and in the process, fucked me over. I didn't come here wanting to revisit that day in front of everyone. While I'll never forget it, images are too much. They're too clear.

I can hear my shallow breaths. They're loud, playing in my ear like a loud, hated song.

Melody stands. "I swear, that's it, Malachi. I didn't include your deceased family. I only wanted to demonstrate that even with the narrative they're pushing about your skin color, that you were still treated like any other Black person in that situation. I wanted everybody to see…"

Silence. My ears process no sound, though I can see her lips still moving. As she speaks, trying to justify her selfish actions, I can't hear anything. I can't feel anything but treachery and fury as a tear slides down her cheek.

This is precisely why people of color struggle to trust white people. Melody including me without my permission is the opposite of allyship. Instead, it's control. Though her intentions may have been good, I, the only Black man in this room, and the one actually victimized by a racist, have been forced into another unwanted position by a white person.

Like every other person of color in this country, I'm tired of having to recover from the traumas brought on by white people. I'm tired of being told by my supposed allies how long to grieve, how to recover from hardships they've never faced, how to prove myself when I shouldn't even have to. I'm sick of having my burdens measured on scales created to diminish me and all that I'm carrying. I'm over being used and discarded and having to forgive those trying to navigate unpaved roads on their journey to allyship.

Mr. Roberts waves his arms in a *look at me* motion, lips moving, but like Melody, I can't hear what he's saying.

Shaking all over, fast, short breaths fill my ears again. I keep my eyes away from the screen. I refuse to potentially enrage myself to the point of no return.

A hand touches my right arm, and in a fast, bird-like movement, I turn and make eye contact with *it*. Just as the black and white film transitioned to color, before my eyes, the room fades to red.

Flames engulf me as we recognize one another, and he immediately steps back, shockingly aware of whom he's standing before once again.

His eyes are still as dark as his soul. Though his hair has been cut, I'll never forget this animal's face. A groom job is not a good enough disguise, not even in the dark.

My eyes move from his face to the Police Academy emblem on his shirt. *A future cop who already has blood on his hands.*

I tremble more aggressively, shake my head, trying to convince myself that this is not possible, that this is a dream, a lucid nightmare that smells and feels all too real.

The thought of him legally armed brings about the fear of more innocents being killed. I foresee black and brown teens gunned down at traffic stops, women of color man-handled and tased for no reason, nonviolent people beaten, handcuffed individuals choked to their deaths. I see him getting away with what he already has, again and again.

Red. Everything around me is the color of bloodshed, but him.

Hot. This theater feels like a furnace.

Terrified. My fear is more consuming than my anger.

Standing before a privileged, bigoted, white officer in the making is one of the most dangerous positions for a Black man to be in.

Hand shaking, arm extended, I see the Glock 9mm in front of me. I feel the trigger behind my index finger. No recollection of unzipping my bag. No memory of turning the safety off.

One shot.

The red subsides as Bennett Dickson's body is thrown into the wall behind him. Like the fresh hole in his shoulder, his black eyes remain open and on me.

I pull, pull, pull. Bang! Bang! Bang!

He goes down, the drum-piercing ringing in my ears nearly taking me down with him.

Still boiling, ears burning, the room red but not as dark as before, I'm over him, the only thing not the color of gore. He reaches up, grabs a hold of my shirt.

Dark red again.

I'm back in a sea of blood, of *their* blood, gagging.

Like before, no remembrance of my brain telling it to, like someone else is operating my body, my arm is stretched, the gun aimed right at his heart.

His body jolts and jolts, high frequency ringing still all I hear.

Paralyzed, I stand, looking from the aimed gun, to his motionless body, and back again.

The color of the room slides from his chest, his shoulder wound, his mouth. Pitch black eyes, once full of evil, now hold nothing. No hate, no sight, no life.

Stuck, head tremoring, I stare till his eyelids hide his once wicked black holes. Feeling here, feeling outside of myself, I peer down at one man, backed by a biased system, who destroyed a whole and happy family.

I step back, the smell of that Friday lingering. I twitch, one ear throbbing, the other stabbed by pain over and over. Unbalanced, too many senses overwhelmed at once, I place my hand over my head, trying to end the rattling. I blink hard, but the room won't go back to the way it was.

Red. More of it. So much of it, I can't see through it.

My head spins. I can't get my bearings.

I'm moving. Legs in motion, swimming through an ocean of blood, without direction.

My head knocks violently. My eardrums feel like they're on the verge of rupture.

I close my eyes, enter darkness, then rub them open, trying to massage away the red.

I'm out. Out of the bloodiness, out of the black, and back in the theater's lobby.

What the fuck? How?

I look around a space I don't recall re-entering. Alone, I stand, my ears still aching, but able to pull in the sound of sirens. I look down, see the blood on my favorite shirt and the 9mm at my feet.

Through the glass, blue and red lights flash. Officers positioned behind their opened doors kneel, guns drawn.

Muddled, I survey everything on the other side of the windows, unclear about so much. No sense of how much time has elapsed. No memory of leaving the presentation room. No understanding of why the gun is on the floor and if that was their order or my choice.

"Malachi," she calls out gently.

I turn toward her voice, see her partially hidden behind the old popcorn counter. Her brown curls stick to her sweaty cheeks. Her extended hands reach out to me, open and shaky.

I step back from the gun, and she steps toward me, her hands now up.

"I'm just going to take the gun, Malachi."

With one swift sweep of my foot, I kick the gun away from me and further away from Melody.

"I need to take the gun so they don't shoot you," she says.

Gun or no gun, I'm dead.

She steps carefully toward the weapon, hands still up. Her bloodshot eyes, full of tears, are on me. "Please," she begs.

My body shudders as she reaches the weapon and drags it with her foot toward the front doors. She cracks the entrance door slightly. "Unarmed!" she yells. "He's unarmed!" She turns to me. "Please put your hands up."

"Step out!" an officer yells back. "Step out. Hands up!"

"Don't shoot him!" She pulls the door open more and kicks the murder weapon outside. Ignoring their instructions, she steps further back into the lobby, at my side.

"Get out," I whisper, but she doesn't hear me. Or maybe she's just ignoring me.

The front door swings open, and ballistic shields enter first with officers behind them.

"Hands up, motherfucker!" an armed officer yells.

Fresh sweat escapes every single one of my pores. Slowly, and unsteadily, I put my hands up.

"Sweetheart, step away from him," the same officer orders.

More officers enter, more obscenities thrown my way, so many guns pointed at me.

"How many hurt?" another officer asks.

"Just one," Melody answers, crying, her voice cracking. "He just snapped, but he didn't hurt any of our classmates. Just that guard. Look, he's complying."

"Get on the fucking floor!" a different officer shouts, as several step toward me in unison, huge guns getting so close to me.

I close my eyes. No need to see my ending. Knowing it's here is enough.

"No!" Melody screams, forcing my eyes to spring open. She moves to stand in front of me, arms stretched out protectively. "He's complying. Put the guns down and just arrest him."

Her small frame stands before me, and like a knot removed from a balloon, releasing the held in air, tensions decrease and their guns lower.

A bald, stocky, brown-skinned officer steps toward Melody and me. With his hands up, he approaches unthreateningly. "I'm going to remove my cuffs from my belt," he says. "No gun drawn. I'm not here to hurt you. Please turn around for me, young man."

I do.

"Hands down and behind your back."

Again, I do as I'm told.

In what feels like a second, my wrists are locked in metal cuffs.

"The suspect has been apprehended," one officer states into his radio.

"You're going to fry for this shit," another says, only inches from me, his sour smelling saliva flying in my face.

The arresting officer grabs a hold of my quivering arm and escorts me out the door, passing officers unafraid to display their disdain for me. Once secured in the back of his vehicle, I peer down at Dickson's blood on my favorite shirt. I stare at a ruined gift I once adored, then turn to look out the window at a safer world.

Out the window, I watch as Melody is surrounded by officers and comforted for what she just went through. Farther up the sidewalk, I spot Nikki, being held back by an officer not dressed in SWAT gear, screaming 'No' hysterically, her gaping eyes full of fear and panic.

153

The arresting officer, the only officer of color I've seen here, reopens my car door. "What's your name, son?"

I don't answer, can't stop reeling and taking in all that's going on.

With her eyes on me through the car window, Melody cries as officers stand at her side, one rubbing her back, offering consolation.

Tears of relief don't fall from my eyes, but I'm grateful to be one of the lucky few. I'm alive, Black, and going to have a trial. Not because I complied. Not because I was unarmed when the police arrived. Because Melody's life is more valuable than mine. I'm alive and in this car because of who stood in front of me. Had Nikki screamed at those officers and jumped in front of me, we both would've been gunned down, but Melody is the race my skin color is. Unlike me, her features don't contradict her complexion, and because of that, she's worthy of protection, of respect, and the ability to have a future. My hands were held up, empty, but countless guns were still aimed at my body. They lowered for one reason. There was no proof that Melody wasn't an accomplice or packing a gun of her own, but they could see the one and only thing they needed to—that she's white.

"Young man, what's your name?" the officer asks again.

The news has printed outright lies, has degraded my murdered family repeatedly, and has disgustingly tried to take something from me that

I'm proud to own. My race. But since so many think I'm lucky and like to believe this skin grants me privilege my family members will never have, let's test their theory.

"Your name, son?"

I make eye contact with him, still sweating, still trembling all over. "You think I could get a burger?" I whisper.

"Say what?" The officer bends to better hear me.

"A burger," I say again.

He stands back up, scoffs lightly. "You know that's not going to happen. Right color, kid. Wrong race."

EPILOGUE

It's been two months since I've seen the sun, the moon, smelled the rain, heard a bird. Instead, my days are spent inside an eight-by-ten-foot concrete box, inhaling what I wish I could go nose blind to.

I originally thought one couldn't be held in solitary confinement for more than thirty days straight, but I guess I understood wrong, or maybe that was simply wishful thinking. I've survived sixty long days in here. I count by the trays. Each day, I've spent alone, listening to the screams of other prisoners and smelling the feces they never scrubbed from my walls.

I never expected jail to be an easy experience. As a matter of fact, I never pictured myself locked up. Yet here I am, experiencing what I wouldn't wish on an enemy. What the guards keep telling me is for *my safety*, is really their way of brutally punishing me for killing who would've become one of their own.

Random knocks on my metal cell door rip me from my already unrestful sleep. I've received trays in which my already oddly colored loaves have been smashed or soiled in strange liquids. I've received letters from Nikki and my family weeks after they were sent. I've listened to other prisoners being taken out to the yard to sit in cages for fresh air, while my cell has been walked past, ignored. What they've been calling safe-keeping has actually been psychological torture, and they've succeeded in breaking me down more and more each day.

Now, desperate and wishing for things I never thought I would, I'd give anything to be a part of this jail's general population, have the ability to breathe in fresh air, and listen to other people, even if they're not interested in talking to me. To feel human again, even like a rejected one, would be a treat. In here, I'm not sure how I feel. Only two months down, and when I'm not showering with a guard watching, I'm locked in this room, sometimes alone, sometimes with who I hope is still just a hallucination.

Visions that appeared every once in a while now haunt me night and day. What began as shadowy colors and glints of light swirling dizzyingly into a silhouette ultimately transformed into a uniformed officer, white and armed, holding a gun larger than my arm.

Firearm locked and loaded, he taunts me, enrages me, confuses and horrifies me during every unwanted visit, no matter how much I tell myself he isn't really here. Never appearing in the hall or shower, I'm convinced he wants me alone when he finally pulls the trigger, something I'm trying to put off, something spending more time out of this room could save me from. But I'm barely ever out, which is why I need today to work out.

Today, the start of day sixty-one, I'm having my first visit. *Hopefully.* I haven't seen Mama in two months, haven't seen Nikki since *that night,* haven't been able to begin the fight Grandma got me so pumped up for. I had expected to see them all a month ago, but the approval took longer than I had hoped. The guards and counselors knew about the delay, but toyed with my feelings for kicks. With the delivery of my breakfast tray that morning, I was told my visit was cleared. Hours of pacing with impatience ended with my heart being crushed. Along with my lunch tray that day came a message. A guard yelled through my door, "Oh man, forgot to tell you. Your visitor sheet hasn't been approved yet." After he walked off, I spent the rest of the day drowning in my own sorrows.

A whole month later, and more than ever, I so badly need to see my mama. I need her to see my face, to see me unbruised, so she knows that while I may be suffering in here, I'm making it without being someone's prison husband or punching bag.

I pace the small space, my eyes on my stained uniform bottoms. The urine stain wasn't made by me. This is how I received them, tainted and putrid. It's what I have to wear to present myself to my mother. When they slid my breakfast through the slot in the door, I tried to ask for a new set, but the slot closed as I fumbled over the first word. Whoever was on the other side laughed loud enough for me to hear as he walked away, leaving me inside someone else's soiled bottoms. Last night, I attempted to wash them in the small, steel sink, but the smell has managed to linger, and my options have run out.

Back and forth, back and forth, back and forth I walk, waiting to hear the lock turn, dreadfully wanting to feel the bracelets tighten around my wrist. Two signs that I'm actually leaving this room.

No clock on the wall to know the exact time. No update as to why I haven't been escorted to the visitation room yet. All I know is, it feels like hours since I've flushed my inedible lunch, and I was supposed to begin my visit at 12:30 p.m. No one has told me that it's been cancelled, so I don't know what to think other than another letdown is headed my way.

I rub my temples as the sharp start of a migraine stabs my left side. I expect them daily now that my photophobia glasses have somehow been "misplaced" by the officers.

Tears well in my eyes, but I wipe them away. They say, *believe and you shall receive.* I believe I'm going to see Mama today. I believe the lifeline I need is going to come through this visit with her and Nikki.

Back and forth, I continue, sweat breaking out all over me, my belly doing somersaults.

"Please, please, please," I cry out quietly. "Please let me out."

The slot in my door opens. On the other side, a stern voice says, "Hands behind your back."

Anxiously, I move to the door, turn my back to it, and hold my wrists together so they can be cuffed through the rectangle space. Secured in my metal bracelets, the door opens.

"Move it. You're late." His blue eyes pierce my light hazel eyes, and in a snobbish head motion, he nods in the direction he wants me to walk.

Late. It's not like I can be sure of the time or come and go as I please. *Asshole.*

Cuffed, I walk past closed metal doors. Screams fill the hall. Locked-in prisoners yell their demands to be let out, to be fed, to know what day it is. I feel their pain, don't know their crimes, but am pretty sure, most of them, if not all, don't deserve to be imprisoned like this.

We hang a right at the corner, and I walk along the wall, following the yellow line as instructed. Through squinted eyes, I try to pull in my surroundings without taking in too much of the corridor's bright light. Another cuffed inmate, several feet in front of me, owned by the DOC just like me, walks defeated with his head lowered, his body dragging against the wall like he'd fall over if it weren't there to support him.

"Left," the correctional officer directs.

161

I turn at the corner of the hall, and at the far end, my eyes land upon the double doors I've been dying to see for months. On the other side, they're in there. Love is in this building, waiting to greet me. The lifeline I begged for, I'm about to receive.

Tears I can't wipe away roll down my face. My stomach flips and flips and flips. I don't know how they're going to react to seeing me in this uniform, in cuffs, smelling of urine, but I hope more than anything that they know my heart is still good. I killed a man. Yes. I wanted him punished for what he did to our family. Yes. But I didn't plan to cross paths with him again. I didn't know I'd see him that night. I didn't consciously plan to shoot him, regardless of the fact that guilt and remorse still haven't hit me. I can't explain how devoid of emotion I am when it comes to the act I committed. I can only process feeling cheated, victimized, and abused by the state that was willing to employ a killer as a cop. Had he been in here, I'd never have seen red, pulled the trigger, and signed my life away.

The correctional officer opens the door to the visitation room, and in the far back corner, sitting side by side at a steel table, holding hands, are my girls. Simultaneously, they both stand. I want to run to them, swoop them both up in my arms, but I know fast movements will get me taken down.

Slowly, I head for their table, passing a couple in a firm embrace, with my unfriendly escort right at my side.

"Where are your glasses?" Nikki asks before I'm even uncuffed.

I stand quietly, surrounded by chatter, as my wrists are freed. Once able to separate my arms, I open them wide, prepared to hug Mama.

The officer holds his arm out in front of me. "No touching."

I turn back to the couple I just saw hug, then make eye contact with Nikki. Silently, we communicate through hurt eyes. Other couples and families are touching. We know that I'm specifically being given this rule for personal reasons.

"Five minutes," The officer says before walking away.

The three of us sit, them on their side of the round table, me alone across from them. Unable to hold it in, we sob.

Weeping and trembling, Mama reaches out, but lets her hands fall to the table. I slightly lift my right hand, but carefully place it back down, dying to touch her, but terrified of what else I'll be deprived of if I do.

I whisper, "Mama."

The bags under her eyes have darkened and are carrying more stress. Her glow, her natural radiance, is still absent. Her natural hair, something she's always taken pride in, is hidden beneath a wig, something she's always been dead set against.

163

Mama brings her hands to her face, covers her tearful eyes, begins quivering incessantly. Nikki, distraught too, rubs Mama's back, but keeps her bawling eyes on me.

"Mama," I whisper again, forcing more tears out of the three of us. "I'm sorry."

"You snapped," Nikki says in a low voice. "You can't apologize for what was out of your control. You lost it. That's what that girl Melody reported."

Melody. My unexpected shield. The confused ally in training. My bullet-proof vest.

"I don't know if they're letting you hear it in here, but the world is not staying quiet about this, Malachi. They want you to get off claiming temporary insanity. Your classmates are saying you stood unresponsive as your teacher repeatedly asked you to sit. Melody said you were glaring at Dickson, shaking all over, and then just suddenly pulled out the gun and started firing while screaming. I guess you must have walked over to him because he somehow grabbed your shirt. After firing the two final shots, you walked out. No one has given an eye-witness account of you standing over him. We only know that because of your shirt. The other kids in there said they hit the floor, hiding behind the seats."

Screaming? I guess it wasn't just them I couldn't hear.

164

I shrug in response to Nikki's words, incapable of detailing exactly what happened either. After realizing who was in the room with me, I was covered in my family's blood again, overwhelmed by the smell, the sight of it.

I know I shot him, and I remember the police showing up, but the details in between are spotty, a sea of red, full of loud breaths, replaced by deafening shots.

I look from Nikki, to my broken Mama, then back to Nikki again.

"Malachi," Nikki calls out gently. "They're protesting everywhere. All races. Albino Lives Matter is a hashtag now. Free Malachi is trending. Your family's names are on the tips of everyone's tongues again. The Black community is posting all over social media that your skin may be white, but you're still Black, and that's why you've been imprisoned and Dickson never was. Big things are happening out in the streets," she tells me. "That girl, Melody, is telling people how you were isolated at school, embarrassed by the teacher daily, and how you never let go of that bag."

I listen, the shock making my hands to spasm, the news briefly drying my helpless tears.

"She talks a lot, Malachi, but her saying that may have really helped us. It's clear that you didn't bring this random backpack to the theater, having never carried it before. Based on what she said, you hugged it all the time, and always had it with you. It doesn't sound like you showed up, displaying

165

unusual behavior, prepared to commit a premeditated crime."

So, there is a fight going on. A fight for me. "Where's Grandma?" I ask, almost inaudibly.

"Talking to a lawyer. There's no way a public defender is going to do what we need them to do. We're getting you out of here."

I shake my head, lean in, and say, "Nikki, I did it. People saw me do it."

"You weren't in your right mind, Malachi."

"Yeah, well, I am the right race to get the worst treatment possible," I whisper.

Mama slaps the table, pulling our eyes to hers. "I'm getting you out of here. You hear me?" she asks, her voice raspier than I've ever heard it. "My son, my only son, is not spending his life in here."

I can't help it. I need to touch my mama, to have some human contact. That voice I haven't heard in so long, that used to calm me mid-panic, that used to motivate me when I didn't want to move, and make me smile when I didn't feel like it, sounds different, but it's the only one that can say those words and make me believe them.

I reach out to her, and Mama reaches to place her hand in mine. I stretch out my other hand, and without hesitation, Nikki places hers in my palm. I close my eyes, squeeze their hands, and try to make a memory of this feeling, of the warmth of their skin.

In just seconds, a full memory not recorded, my right arm is grabbed, and I'm pulled away from my loves. "You're done. Let's go," the officer says harshly.

Mama stands. "I mean it, baby. We're fighting for you, Malachi! We won't stop until we bring you home."

"Escort them out," the officer holding me tells another.

"I love you," Mama and Nikki say in unison.

God, I love y'all too.

As I'm cuffed again and directed back to the only place on Earth I'd choose Hell over, I exhale, not relieved, but no longer feeling like I'm rotting away. There's a world of people fighting for me, including the strongest woman I know. My mama. And with that, I'm given something most Black people in prison can't hold onto. Hope.

ACKNOWLEDGMENTS

First and foremost, I must give thanks to God. On my darkest days, you give me light. On my most frustrating days, my conversations with you bring me peace. On those days when I doubt myself, you bless me with the confidence I need to trust my creative instincts. My faith grounds me, strengthens me, and uplifts my spirit. I could never say "Thank You" enough.

Kayla, my first born, my best friend, and the one who proved to me that love at first sight is absolutely real, you have no idea what you do for me. You drive me crazy, and right now, you're probably wearing something of mine that I won't ever see in my closet again. But no matter how much you frustrate me, you are the reason I smile. You are the most amazing daughter in the world, and without even realizing it, you motivate me every day. I feel unbelievably privileged to be your mother, and I want my successes to be proof that you can achieve anything your heart desires, no matter how unreal it seems to others or how long it takes you to get there. Claim what you want and take the first step, knowing your biggest cheerleader will always be here to support and celebrate you. I love you, doll, to infinity and beyond. (You're smiling right now because you just read that in my horrible Buzz Lightyear voice.)

Kaden, my love, my other bestie, my goofball, and my favorite writing buddy, you bring me so much joy. You are my ball of energy, my unpredictable prankster, and though you often make me feel like I'm going nuts, you have no idea how much you inspire me and keep me motivated. No question, I have the most loving son, and I thank God for you every day. Your huge heart and care for others truly makes my soul sing. You don't know it yet, kiddo, but you are going to make this world a much better place. You are not only a fantastic writer, but you've wanted to help people before you could even speak clearly. It is an honor to be your mother. Making you proud is one of my greatest goals, and I can't wait to see how far our writing takes us. I love you beyond words, my only son, even though you think you're my father.

Kahina "Bubbs" Haynes, thank you for letting me talk your ear off about this story, and even more importantly, for being my sister and hair stylist. Having you in my life makes things all the more exciting and unpredictable. What can I say, you're just fucking incredible!

My beta-readers, Chelsea, Stephanie, and Sophia, endless thanks for your helpful feedback. It was all so helpful.

Dominique Scott, we've worked together for years, and I see us partnering again on many more projects. You're a fabulous line editor who never aims to take my voice away. Thank you so much!

Kaitlin Travis, I am so grateful to have found you. You're such a skilled proofreader, and without a doubt, I'd love to work together again. Thank you so much.

Julie Overpeck, I can't thank you enough. They say, "trust your gut", and I'm so glad I did. I knew I needed another set of eyes, and you caught so much we all missed. Thank you for being my final proofreader. I am so grateful to have found you.

Molly, you already know how obsessed I am with your beautiful work. You gave my book a face, and I love how this came out. As I said before, I hope we get to work together from here on out, on all of my future projects. I can't thank you enough for your patience, kindness, professionalism, and talent.

Last, and most certainly not least, thank you to all of my family and friends. The support will never go unnoticed or unappreciated, and my love for you guys will never die. Y'all truly have my heart!

ABOUT THE AUTHOR

Tammy Ferebee, author of three previously published books, lives and writes in Baltimore, Maryland. She is a dedicated mother and enjoys spending time with her two beautiful children. When she's not cheering her kids on from the sidelines at a sporting event, she's likely overcooking a new vegan dish, cozied up with a good read, or burning the midnight oil working on her next literary masterpiece.

While writing is one of Tammy's deepest passions, helping others is what makes her soul sing. Tammy volunteers regularly, participates in several humanitarian efforts throughout each year, and has recently discovered a love for Reiki: both giving and receiving.

Connect with Tammy Ferebee:

Website: www.tammyferebee.com

Instagram: @authortammyferebee

Twitter: www.twitter.com/tammyferebee

Facebook: www.facebook.com/Tammy-Ferebee-1030336110351033/

Made in the USA
Middletown, DE
26 May 2022